THE BADMAN'S DAUGHTER

When Daniel Cliff arrives in Ranch Town, he discovers the settlement is caught in the stranglehold of a brutal tyrant, and refuses to take sides. That is until the spirited Charlotte 'Charlie' Wells, heir to the Crooked-W ranch, crosses his path. When she offers him the chance to help her right the wrongs being rained down on the town, he has no qualms about using her troubles to further his own ambitions. However, Charlie is no pawn in a man's game — and nobody is going to stand in her way . . .

Books by Terry James
in the Linford Western Library:

LONG SHADOWS
ECHOES OF A DEAD MAN
GHOSTS OF BLUEWATER CREEK

TERRY JAMES

THE BADMAN'S DAUGHTER

Complete and Unabridged

LINFORD
Leicester

First published in Great Britain in 2016 by
Robert Hale
an imprint of The Crowood Press
Wiltshire

First Linford Edition
published 2018
by arrangement with
The Crowood Press
Wiltshire

*A catalogue record for this book is available
from the British Library.*

ISBN 978–1–4448–3885–5

Published by
F. A. Thorpe (Publishing)
Anstey, Leicestershire

Set by Words & Graphics Ltd.
Anstey, Leicestershire
Printed and bound in Great Britain by
T. J. International Ltd., Padstow, Cornwall

This book is printed on acid-free paper

With thanks to
Leigh A

1

When Daniel Cliff entered Ranch Town, he knew there would be eyes on him. In a place like this, strangers never went unnoticed.

The noise and bustle inside the Lucky Diamond saloon didn't abate for even one breath of time when he rode by. Nobody disturbed their revelry to wonder at the newcomer's late arrival. At close to eleven o'clock on a Saturday night, men gambled at Faro, Black Jack and low stakes poker, women giggled and while a small band played jaunty tunes, cowhands danced with pretty girls whose only plan was to part them from their hard-earned wages.

When he reached the Good Night Hotel, he stepped easily out of the saddle and tied his grey horse at the hitch rail. After loosening the cinch, he paused to once again survey his surroundings. Besides the saloon, everywhere was dark and quiet. Even inside the hotel, Daniel could have been forgiven for thinking the place was abandoned. The shabby foyer offered nothing more than a layer of dust, a sagging sofa and a desk.

Daniel's boot heels made a pronounced clicking sound as he approached the old woman dozing behind the reception. Stifling a yawn, she turned up the lamp, a frown deepening the lines in her weathered face as she looked him over.

It didn't bother him. He knew he was a little bit tall, a little bit skinny, and his high-crowned, wide-brimmed hat shadowed most of his face. A dusty bandanna obscured the rest.

Her gaze rested on the gun, holstered against his hip. It wouldn't tell her much since most travelling men carried one. The scowl she gave him as her appraisal moved upwards again told him she couldn't quite make up her mind about him. It also reminded him that while his boots, canvas trousers and corduroy jacket were in good shape, his hair hadn't seen a barber in a while. The bandanna rasped over three-day-old stubble as he lowered it. When he gave her a smile that usually put people at their ease, his face felt stiff.

Still she continued to stare through narrowed eyes.

'Evening, ma'am.' His voice sounded raspy after hours of inactivity. 'Do you have a room?'

'They call me Ma, not ma'am, and as you can plainly see, young man, this is a hotel so it makes sense there would be rooms. As to whether I can fix you up with one, that depends. It'll cost you fifty cents a night, paid up front, and another twenty-five cents for breakfast in the dining room between seven and nine. How does that suit you?'

He nodded his approval, again flashing her an easy smile designed to counter any remaining doubt.

With only a slight hesitation, she slid the register towards him. 'And when you're ready to leave, I can pack you up something to see you on your way.'

He chuckled. She was a tough cookie. No doubt she had to be to survive.

'Ma, is that your way of telling me to get out of town?'

For a split second, her expression registered confusion, maybe a little fear, and as she floundered for an answer his grin deepened.

'Don't worry, I'm not looking for trouble.' But a little mischief never did any harm. 'That's not to say it won't come looking for me. Let's start with one night and see what happens.'

The wink he gave her, as he handed over a dollar, apparently cast away enough doubt and she invited him to sign the register. When he was finished, she checked the name and handed him a key on a wooden fob with the number 3 scorched into it.

'For an extra twenty-five cents I'll put your horse in the lean-to at the back and give him a few oats.'

He glanced at the clock on the wall. 'Is it too late to take him to the livery stable?'

'Don't matter what the time is. The livery burned down two days ago. Probably shouldn't say this but you might want to sleep in your clothes, just in case this place goes the same way.'

2

Charlotte 'Charlie' Wells breathed deep and shook her head as she looked along the length of fence that separated the Crooked-W ranch from its neighbour. Posts had been pulled down in several places, the wire in between snapped and trampled into the ground. Looking across the desolate stretch of north pasture it was easy to estimate the number of Lazy J cattle that had been driven through.

And there was no doubt they had been driven through, by at least two riders who had returned the same way, making no attempt to disguise their tracks.

'What did you find?' her cousin asked, riding forward to join her.

'Nothing new. Just Johnson up to his usual games.' She mounted her waiting horse. 'We should get back to the house.'

Her cousin leaned over in the saddle to examine the tracks. When he straightened up, he pushed back his coat and rested his hand on the six-gun holstered at his waist.

'I've a mind to go over there now and — '

Charlie grabbed his arm. 'Just leave it, Billy. You can't go over there and start throwing accusations or anything else. You're not a gunfighter and that's what you'd be riding into the middle of. Those men with Val Johnson, they'd kill you on sight.'

He scowled at her, obviously knowing she was right but too het up to admit it. At seventeen, he was two years younger than her, the whiskers on his chin barely more than peach fuzz, his temper unfettered by the weight of experience.

'Come on, let's go. It's nearly suppertime and I'm hungry. Besides, your pa told us to stay out of the north pasture. We shouldn't even be here.'

He had looked ready to agree but

now he huffed. 'Pa said. That's all he ever does is talk. That fall last year didn't just break his legs. It broke his spirit. We need to be doing something. We can't just stand around here and wait for Johnson to roll right over us. You and me together, we could talk some sense into him. You know I'm right.'

Charlie frowned the way she always did when he said things she didn't want to hear. 'You shouldn't be so hard on him. He's just doing what he thinks is best. Nobody wants an all out war, not even you. So we have to repair a few fences and round up some Lazy J cattle from time to time, it's better than burying dead men. Besides, what do you think I can say that you haven't?'

'You can reason with him. He listens to you more than he does to me. You're more like a son to him than I am.'

She shrugged, uncomfortable with the odd truth, yet unable to deny it. Dressed in worn stovepipe chaps over blue jeans, a red shirt open at the neck and a short leather coat, at a distance she could easily pass for a cowhand. And since his accident, her Uncle Tom had been handing over more responsibility to her. His name might be behind everything, but she was the one running things day-to-day.

'Come on, Charlie,' Billy cajoled. 'When we came to live with you and your pa, you were as tough as rawhide, always looking for a fight.'

'And that's why he left me here, so that I could learn to be more civilized.'

'But you still miss it, don't you? Your old life? That's why you practise with that old six-shooter when you think no one's watching.'

There was no point denying it. She told herself she rode away from the house to shoot at bottles and cans so that her uncle didn't get to hear about it, but maybe Billy was right.

He slapped his thigh. 'You do miss it.'

'I miss my pa, not the life I had with him,' she said, flatly. 'Listen, Billy, you want to believe I'm still rough and tumble Charlie, but I'm not. I'm a woman now. My thinking's different. I want different things.'

'You just think you do.'

She thrust out her hand so he could see it. 'Look, I'm shaking over a broken-down fence. Do you still think I'm tough?'

'It doesn't mean you're scared. It just means you know as well as I do that this isn't the end of it. The town's already as good as his. Johnson's just expanding his territory and if we don't want to get swallowed up . . . '

Billy's glare held firm until Charlie threw up her hands in mock-surrender.

'All right, I'm not going to win this argument now, so I'll think about it later, but,' she added, teasing him, 'only because you're my favourite cousin, Billy Mason.'

'I'm your only cousin.' He broke into a grin as he neck-reined his horse in the direction of home. 'And by the way, I know you're a woman but you are still rough and tumble. I've seen you with that broncbuster, Al, when you think no one's looking. Has he asked you to marry him yet?'

She grinned.

'So he has.' He gave her a sly sideways look. 'Have you told him about your pa and the Crooked-W?'

'No, but it won't make any difference to him.'

He frowned. 'What about my pa? You marryin' is going to mean a big change for him. How do you think he's going to take it? He's been boss of the Crooked-W for a long time.'

She had been wondering that herself. Maybe that's why she hadn't told him yet.

'You said it yourself,' she said, 'he's hardly been interested in the place since his accident. Maybe he'll take the money that's coming to him and go do something different.'

'So you've made up your mind then? You're definitely going to marry Al and take over the Crooked-W?'

She nodded. 'Are you happy about it?'

'Hell, yes. I couldn't be happier.' He laughed. 'Well, maybe I will be when I see the look on Johnson's face when he finds out who he's dealing with.'

3

'I learned my trade when I was no more than a boy and I've been perfecting it ever since. I guarantee this'll be the best shave you've ever had or your money back,' the old barber bragged.

He lifted the hot towel away from Daniel's face, almost immediately massaging soap into the softened bristles and opened pores.

'The trick is,' he continued, after cleaning his hands and picking up the cut-throat razor, 'not to let the lather dry.'

Deftly, with his left hand, he stretched the skin just forward of Daniel's ear, then with his right, placed the razor flat against Daniel's cheek and lifted the blade to the required angle.

'Now you just sit nice and still,' the barber said, applying a little pressure on the first downward stroke.

Feeling comfortable and relaxed, Daniel closed his eyes to concentrate fully on the feel of the blade moving swiftly and precisely over his skin. It was a luxury he didn't usually afford himself, but he wanted to make a good first impression.

As he applied a second layer of soap, the barber said, 'You're new in town. Are you passing through or looking for work?'

'Depends.'

'On anything in particular?'

Daniel grinned. 'On what I find.'

'What are you looking for?'

Daniel shrugged.

'Well, if you're looking for a job, I'd recommend the Lazy J.'

'I'm no cowpuncher.'

The barber's eyes moved towards the outline of the gun visible through the sheet. He wiped his hands and picked up the cut-throat razor.

'Maybe there's something else you're good at.'

Daniel let the suggestion linger for a

few seconds, watching as the man ran the blade expertly up and down the leather strop.

'I hear they're a tough outfit,' he said at last.

'Mr Johnson's ambitious. Some people don't like that.'

'Is it true he takes what he wants?'

The barber held up his hands, as though warding off evil. 'They're strong words. Don't let anybody from the Lazy J hear you using them.'

'No offence intended.'

'And I take none,' he said, preparing to position the blade against Daniel's cheek. 'But others might.'

'I'm just repeating what I heard along the trail, trying to get both sides of the story, you might say.'

'Sensible, I'm sure, but dangerous. Like I said, Mr Johnson's an ambitious man. People push and he pushes back.' The barber started his second shave, this time against the hair growth. 'Do you know what I mean?'

'Uh huh.'

'That's worth bearing in mind if you're thinking about staying around.'

After he had finished shaving and rinsing, the barber whipped off the sheet that had covered Daniel over, and waved at the display of tonic bottles, oils and pomades lined up within reach on a long marble counter.

Daniel ran his fingers over his skin, liking the smooth, clean feel of it, and shook his head. 'I never had two shaves in one sitting before.'

'It's very popular with the ladies.'

Daniel grinned and handed over the previously agreed fifty cents, wondering how many ladies frequented a barber's, but let the comment pass as his gaze strayed to the street where two men were heading towards the shop. One took a seat against the wall outside, the other entered. Average in height, with short hair and a beard, and wearing a smart grey suit and polished shoes, he looked like a respectable middle-aged businessman.

But Daniel would be the first to

admit that looks could be deceptive and, as he moved closer, his lined face and hard mouth beneath piercing green eyes betrayed the otherwise refined exterior. When he spoke, his voice rumbled like a distant storm, offering no immediate insight into his disposition.

'I heard we had a new arrival in town.'

Daniel noticed the way he held his left arm slightly shy of his side, and the bulge inside his coat. He had heard of men wearing their belt holster slung over the shoulder and across the chest, Mexican bandits and the like, but this was the first time he had come across it.

'My name's Val Johnson.'

His hard green stare seemed to cut right through Daniel, skewering with an intensity that bordered on insanity. Long seconds passed before he blinked, and even then the action was slow and precise. Already Daniel imagined having nightmares about it.

'I didn't catch your name,' he said, breaking his trance-like stare to glance at the Smith & Wesson, worn on the hip and tied against Daniel's thigh. 'But you seem like a man I should know.'

Daniel allowed himself a second to breathe before he introduced himself. 'Daniel Smith.'

'Well, Mr Smith, are you looking for work?'

'It seems to be a common misconception.'

Johnson raised an eyebrow. 'Misconception? That's a fancy word for understanding, isn't it?' He didn't wait for an answer. 'Maybe I read you wrong but perhaps you could humour me. What line of work are you in?'

His brusque attitude bordered on belligerent, and was probably intended to unnerve, but Daniel had his wits about him now.

'I'm sure you read me right,' he said, calmly. 'Helping people mainly.'

It was a deliberately ambiguous answer intended to intrigue, and

Johnson's eyes narrowed as he considered the connotations.

'Maybe we could help each other,' he said at last. He settled himself into the chair Daniel had recently vacated, and closed his eyes. 'Come and find me when you make up your mind.'

Stepping into the street, Daniel stopped as the midday sun momentarily blinded him. As he adjusted the brim of his hat, he was sure he could feel Johnson's gaze on his back, but as much as he felt the need to turn around, he didn't.

4

The town was quiet during the day. People moved around, carrying out their business but no one seemed to linger on the streets. Women simply nodded an acknowledgement to one another, not stopping to gossip. Men worked without resting.

In the evening, Daniel headed to the Lucky Diamond. Only a fancy beaded curtain separated the private gaming room in the rear from the hustle and bustle of the main barroom, but the atmosphere couldn't have been more different. While music played, glasses clinked and flirtatious laughter floated on the air in the smoke-filled outer room, in here men with tight faces and steady hands considered cards that could make or break them.

Daniel slipped in hoping to find an open seat in a friendly game, but the

Fancy Dan, two suited gents and couple of young cowhands showed no signs of resigning their positions. When he entered, a measured look from the dealer was followed by a subtle nod that said if he was staying he should move back and make room.

Beer in hand, he found a place against the wall where a couple of other gents in suits appeared to be waiting. He realized within minutes that the game was too rich for his blood. Why Ma had recommended the place he wasn't sure, but the drama unfolding at the table made him wish he had stayed at the hotel.

The cowhand, Scott, the dealer called him, wiped his palm on the front of his black leather vest, licked his lips and counted the pile of money sitting in front of him. With a smirk, he pushed forward his bet and tried to fondle the blonde girl who had just distributed a round of drinks and now stepped back to watch the game.

'Raise twenty,' he drawled.

Four of the remaining players folded leaving only one to challenge. When he didn't immediately respond, the dealer was quick to prompt him.

'Your call, Billy.'

The kid sitting opposite Scott, who barely looked old enough to shave, eyed the cards on the table. A pair of deuces-eight for him. A pair of queens-eight for his opponent whose piercing green eyes sparkled with arrogance and the effects of too much whiskey.

And then there was the pot that must be worth at least a hundred dollars.

Daniel saw the saloon girl flash Billy a look that said he shouldn't play the hand. But judging by the way the kid eyed Scott's pile of notes, the pot and his own stack of money, he was considering it. After a few seconds' deliberation, he counted out the twenty, then another twenty and placed it all in the centre of the table.

'Your call,' he said, easing back in his seat.

Daniel couldn't recall the last time he had seen a man's eyes actually gleam, but Scott's did. It wasn't hard to know what he was thinking. A pair of queens against a pair of deuces. A pot big enough to afford bragging rights for quite a while. He could hardly push his remaining money forward fast enough.

Billy swiped at the sweat beading his forehead then matched the bet.

Without looking at either player, the dealer dealt the last cards.

Eights for each of them.

'Yes!' Scott leaned in to scrape up the winnings. 'Yet another victory for the Lazy-J. When are you Crooked-W boys gonna realize you just can't win, and get the Hell out of town?'

Daniel pulled himself up straighter. What were the chances of running into Billy Mason, assuming it was him, this soon?

Silently, he thanked Ma for recommending the place.

Meanwhile, the saloon girl leaned

forward to stay Scott's hand. 'It isn't over 'til we see what else he's got.'

Scott glared at her and sneered. 'And just who the Hell asked for your opinion?' He slurred his words, as the whiskey and the euphoria of a big win took effect. 'Why don't you go upstairs and warm the bed for me like a good little whore?'

Whether she intended to slap his face playfully or in earnest, Daniel couldn't be sure, but Scott's reflexes were sharp despite his heavy drinking. His fingers clamped around her wrist before she made contact, a vicious twist bending her to his will before a violent backhand sent her reeling against the wall.

The two men beside Daniel pressed in against him, blocking any move he might have made in her defence. The dealer grabbed Billy's gun hand, stopping him before he could do anything.

'There'll be no shooting in my place. I made the rules plain before you two sat in.' He slackened his grip. 'If you want to show your cards, then go ahead. If you don't, then settle down.'

Picking herself up, the girl nodded at Billy. Apart from a flush to her cheeks and a trickle of blood from a split lip, she looked all right.

Billy took a loud deep breath then flipped over his hole card.

Two of hearts.

Scott stared at the full house mocking him from across the table. He reached for his bottle of whiskey and gulped the whole lot down, wiping his mouth with the back of his hand before turning over the unseen card before him.

An ace.

Daniel realized he was holding his breath at about the same time as everyone else. The sudden release of air was audible even over the unrelenting cacophony coming from the barroom.

Billy swayed as he stood and slapped his hat on his head. 'That's me finished for the night.' He started stuffing money into his pockets. 'I'm wise enough to know I used up all my luck on that hand.'

Dumbly, Scott stared at his cards, then watched as they were shuffled back into the deck. 'I'm not losing that money to you,' he growled.

Billy grinned. 'You already did. I guess luck doesn't play by your rules.'

'What's that supposed to mean?' Scott rose unsteadily to his feet. 'Are you calling me a cheat?'

The abrupt change from stunned defeat to angry affront didn't seem to surprise anyone as they shuffled backwards in their seats.

'If you are, I guess that hand would make you the worst one that ever lived,' Billy said.

Scott studied the faces around the table, but no one seemed eager to get involved, finding ways to avert their eyes from his. At last, his gaze settled back on Billy.

'You think you're better than me, don't you?'

Billy didn't bother looking up as he

gathered in his winnings. 'I can't say I've given it any thought.'

'Seems to me a man would need a high opinion of himself to bet a pair of twos against a pair of queens. Either that or he knows something about the deck.'

However unfounded, it was obvious where his accusation was heading. He was a man backed into a corner, looking for someone to blame for his bad luck.

Despite having a smart mouth, Billy held up his hands, refusing to be drawn into a fight. 'What can I say? I like deuces.' He chuckled. 'And tonight, the deuces liked me. If you've got a problem with the deck, you should take it up with Mr Brady here.'

Puffing on a fat cigar, the dealer raised an eyebrow but continued to shuffle the cards. Beside Daniel, the men who he had assumed were merely watching the game straightened up and focussed on Scott.

'My quarrel ain't with you, Brady. It's with him!'

Scott tried for his gun, but the girl stumbled into him, throwing him off balance. Before he could regain his composure, Brady's men crowded in on both sides.

'I think it's time you called it a night, Scott,' the saloon owner said. 'When your pa took a stake in this place, he promised me there'd be no more trouble.'

Scott considered his next move, looking again at the faces around him, each one tense with expectation. Finally, he raised his hands and backed away.

'Enjoy your luck while it lasts, Billy. One way or another, your days around here are numbered.' He grinned, as something seemed to occur to him. 'And say hello to Charlie for me.'

So far, the quarrel hadn't concerned Daniel. He had seen hot heads letting off steam before, but now he moved his beer to his other hand.

'Tell her I said she looks real nice in those new pants she's been wearing.'

Scott traced a woman's figure in the air.

Daniel's fingers started to curl into a fist, but he held back.

'I bet she looks even better out of them.'

'You filthy sonofabitch.'

The table rocked, threatening to tip over completely as Billy catapulted across it, sending men, money and drinks flying in every direction. One of Brady's heavies managed to grab his arm, thrusting it up his back and slamming him down across the gaming table while his partner shoved Scott out through the beaded curtain.

'I'll kill you Scott Johnson. You go near — '

The man restraining him ground Billy's face into the green baize as though he were stubbing out a cigarette, stifling whatever else he intended to say.

'Take it easy, Billy,' Brady advised.

As Scott's laughter mingled into the revelry of the other patrons, Billy's struggles weakened against the brute strength of his captor, until finally his body went limp.

Daniel eased his palm away from the grip of his gun.

'Are you done now?' Brady asked. 'Can I tell Sloane to let you up?'

Somehow, he managed to nod, contorting his face into a grotesque caricature. When Sloane let him up, he leaned against the table, one hand pressed against his reddened cheek.

'You need to calm down,' Brady said. 'Talk like that could get you killed easy as drawing breath.'

'You heard what he said,' Billy argued.

'All I heard . . . ' He looked around at each man at the table. 'All any of us heard, was a man passing on his regards.'

'Yeah, I guess you would say that now you're a Johnson man. Now you're all Johnson men.'

Brady's mouth tightened into a white line, his eyes narrowing as he concentrated on shuffling the cards. 'If that's what you think, don't come in here again, Billy. And tell your pa to keep the rest of the Crooked-W boys away from the Lucky Diamond.'

Billy opened his mouth to speak but instead snatched up the last of his winnings. Daniel edged forward so that when Billy barged past Brady's men, the kid bumped into him.

Beer splashed over both of them.

'Sorry, mister,' Billy said.

For a second, their eyes met. Close up the kid was even younger than Daniel had first thought, eighteen maybe. The anger that fuelled his temper didn't quite reach his wide blue eyes as he flinched before he could stop himself.

'It's only beer. Buy me another and maybe we'll forget about the shirt.'

5

In contrast to the Lucky Diamond, the Steer's Hide was a quiet, shabby place with thick sawdust on the floor and planks thrown across a couple of barrels to serve as a bar. On the wall behind the barkeep, where there should have been a mirror, someone had painted the words *No Fighting*. The few tables scattered around the room were mostly unoccupied, the establishment's four other customers being content to gather around one table where an oldster was dealing Blackjack.

When Daniel and Billy entered, the barkeep didn't ask what they wanted. He just handed each of them a shot glass, and held out one hand for payment while he waited to pour a dirty-looking liquid with the other.

'How much for the bottle?' Daniel asked.

'Fifty cents. No refunds.'

As Billy handed over the payment, Daniel's insides churned at the thought of drinking the cheap liquor. Almost gingerly, he carried the bottle to a table in the corner. Seating himself with his back to the wall, he splashed whiskey into each glass. He almost winced when Billy gulped his straight down.

'Sorry about your shirt,' Billy said, stifling a choking cough with the back of his hand.

Daniel refreshed the empty glass. 'I've got another.'

He brought his own glass up, but the stink of the whiskey, if that's what it really was, made him lower it without taking a taste. The kid had no such qualms and Daniel slid the bottle across to him, watching while he poured another. Then he waited for him to drink it.

'That was some hand you played back there.'

'It was, wasn't it? I thought my head was going to explode when I turned over that deuce.'

'I thought the other fella's was. He sure didn't like losing.'

'No, sir, he didn't but he needed to be taught a lesson. And not just about how to play cards.' He pulled a half-smoked cigarette from his pocket then feeling around again brought out a match and lit it. 'If Brady hadn't set his man on me I'd have . . . ' His gaze had become distant, but now it snapped back to Daniel. 'I guess I should watch what I say since you're new in town. Maybe we should introduce ourselves before I start running my mouth off. I'm Billy Mason of the Crooked-W.'

'Daniel Smith.'

Billy seemed to hesitate before deciding to speak. 'Do you mind if I ask you a question?'

'It depends.'

'On what?'

Daniel swirled the whiskey around in his glass, watching it touch the lip without spilling. 'What it is.'

Billy had started to pour another

drink and it splashed onto the table as his eyes moved towards the gun visible inside Daniel's open coat.

'Are you working for Johnson?'

It sounded like the portent of a challenge. Maybe the kid planned it to come out that way, or maybe it was the whiskey talking. Either way, Daniel had been around enough drunks to know that even the most agreeable could turn hostile with the tip of a glass.

'No,' he said, leaving no room for misunderstanding.

Billy visibly relaxed. 'Sorry, but I had to ask. If you stick around town long enough, you'll understand why.'

'I think I already might. I heard about the livery stable. Has your outfit had any trouble?'

'Some. Nothing we can't handle.' Billy took several deep draws on his cigarette as it started to die. 'But it's only a matter of time.'

'Have you got enough men working for you to handle it?'

'Why, are you looking for a job?' he

asked, sounding hopeful.

'I'm no cowpuncher.'

'I didn't think you were. I could put a word in with my cousin Charlie, if you're interested. She does all the hiring and firing.'

'A woman?'

Billy chuckled. 'Not just any woman. She can ride and shoot and hammer and nail as good as any man I know, although she tries to hide it.'

'And men take their orders from her?'

'She's earned a lot of respect. Since my pa had his accident, she's probably the only thing been holding the Crooked-W together.'

Daniel's gaze strayed to the doorway where two men had entered. One he recognized as Val Johnson. The other, who made his way to stand with his back against the bar, Daniel could hazard a guess was the infamous Ralph Stanton whose reputation as a gunslick remained intact despite him losing an arm in a botched robbery.

Beneath the table, Daniel loosened the Smith & Wesson in its holster, leaving his hand on his thigh.

After a quick look around, Johnson approached them. His stance was such that he wasn't facing Daniel or Billy directly, yet he managed to address them both with equal intent.

'I've been looking for you.'

The spilled whiskey reached Daniel's fingertips as it crept across the table. He touched his tongue to the back of his teeth, craving a drink to moisten it.

Johnson reached towards his pocket, cocking an eye at Daniel. 'No need to touch that gun, Mr Smith.'

Slowly, he pulled out an envelope, straightened it and handed it to Billy. 'Give this to your pa. Tell him I'll ride over tomorrow to discuss terms.'

'I'll save you the time.' Billy shoved it away. 'We're not interested in your terms.'

'Are you the legal owner of the Crooked-W?'

Billy frowned. 'I can speak for the brand.'

'I said, are you the legal owner?'

Billy's eyes narrowed.

'I didn't think so.' Johnson tossed the envelope in Billy's face. 'Now be a good cowpoke and give this to the man in charge.'

Billy rose as quickly as the colour in his cheeks but Johnson's backhand slammed him down into his seat.

Daniel's glance found Stanton, a drink standing untouched on the bar next to him. He looked relaxed, disinterested almost, but in the next instant, his pistol appeared in his hand as if it had never been anywhere else. His fixed gaze said that Daniel would be his first victim if trouble started.

Daniel willed the kid to stop talking, but even with his eyes tearing up and struggling to focus, his mouth just kept moving.

'You'll never get your hands on the Crooked-W.'

'I'd say that's business between me and your pa.'

'It'll never happen.' Billy laughed.

'There's no way my pa would make a deal for the Crooked-W. It just ain't possible.'

'Anything's possible.' Johnson smiled condescendingly. 'Most men can recognize an opportunity if it's presented the right way.'

'If you're talking to my pa, all the bells and whistles in the world won't do you any good.'

Johnson looked around the room at the faces turned in fearful anticipation, then smiled indulgently as he asked, 'Why, what are you going to do about it?'

'Nothing.'

Billy spread his arms wide, away from the six-shooter at his waist.

Daniel released his breath, but his relief was short-lived.

'Except tell you the Crooked-W doesn't belong to him. Never has. Never will. My pa's just a glorified ranch foreman. He doesn't own any part of it.' Billy's eyes glistened with satisfaction. 'Not a horse, not a saddle, not a blade of grass.'

'Nice try kid. I checked with the bank. There's no mortgage on the place. Never has been.'

Billy chuckled. 'That's because the Crooked-W was here long before civilization arrived.'

The taunt seemed to rattle Johnson. He had been sure of his facts when he entered, now that certainty was being eroded.

'Supposing, just supposing, I believe you and he ain't the owner, then who is?'

Coolly, Billy pushed back the envelope. 'Nobody you want to tangle with.'

Daniel's fingers twitched, whether with expectation or fear, he couldn't have said.

Johnson laughed. 'You're full of bull, kid. I'll speak to your pa myself.' He snatched back the envelope and slipped it inside his coat, signalling Stanton towards the door. 'Tell him to expect me.'

With the doors still swinging on their

sagging leather hinges, Billy pulled his chair back up to the table. He reached for the bottle and shakily poured himself another drink.

'You should take it easy with that stuff,' Daniel remarked.

'Probably, but like the man said . . . ' Billy shuddered as he swallowed it down. 'I'm just a cowpoke. Who the Hell cares what I say?'

6

The next day, Daniel opened his eyes to the semi-darkness and listened. Except for the loud snoring coming from the next room, everything was quiet. Easing himself to a sitting position, he stretched the knots out of his back then pulled on his boots. He hadn't undressed. Maybe he'd been too tired, or maybe Ma's warning had stuck with him.

A cool waft of air rushed in against the stuffiness when he forced the window open. Leaning out, he looked both ways along the street. It was still too dark to see much, but the quiet and stillness gave it an eerie, uninviting feel.

The window groaned when he shut it, rattling the wall and the washstand that leaned against it. He heard water slosh and felt around to steady the pitcher and basin. He hadn't bothered to light a lamp when he entered, knowing he only had to negotiate a few steps from the door to the bed. The water was a pleasant surprise.

He struck a match to see the face of the gold-cased watch he kept in his vest pocket, using the last of its light to check the state of the water.

It was 5.30.

It looked clean.

Still an hour-and-a-half until breakfast. Maybe if he asked nicely, he could at least scare up a cup of coffee.

Minutes later, the third step from the top creaked as he descended the stairs. Ma looked up, her frown dissolving into surprise and lifting into a smile when she recognized him.

'The time you and Billy got in, I didn't expect to see you up this early,' she said.

'I could say the same. Don't you sleep?'

She chuckled. 'I can sleep when I'm dead. Are you hungry?'

'I wouldn't say no, if you're offering.'

She blew out the lamp on the desk and pushed back her seat, a once plush lounge chair that looked oddly out of place in its surroundings. 'If you don't mind eating in the kitchen, I can rustle up some ham and eggs and coffee strong enough to stand a spoon in, if that's the way you like it.'

She led him into the kitchen, a clean and airy room with a large scrubbed table flanked by two benches worn to a dark patina. Faded yellow curtains covered the window and a dresser filled with china lined the wall. A chair, similar to the one she had recently vacated, sat beside the fire, which crackled in the grate.

'Homely, ain't it? Not what you'd expect when you come in the front. I don't usually invite people back here.'

'Why'd you make an exception for me?'

It took fresh scrutiny and a few seconds for her to decide on her answer. 'You clean up well. Sit and don't make me regret it.'

She sang while she cooked, nothing he recognized, but a sweet melody all the same. It seemed at odds with her outwardly gruff attitude. The plate of food she placed before him was hot and plentiful. It didn't matter that the bacon was fatty and the eggs runny, because the biscuits more than made up for it. As for the coffee . . .

He stifled a yawn and accepted a refill.

'You look like you could do with some more shut-eye. I know the beds in this place ain't what they used to be. You're welcome to try that chair for a couple of hours. You can take it from me, it's as comfortable as it looks.'

He grinned. 'Do you think I could sleep after two cups of that coffee?'

'At the very least you could rest your eyes for a while. Maybe we could even get to know one another a little better.'

'It's a tempting offer.'

'So what's stopping you?'

This was turning into a game of cat and mouse. Did she know who he was, or was she just guessing?

'You don't strike me as the trusting type and yet here I am sitting in your kitchen with a full belly and the offer of a comfortable chair by a warm fire. I'm just wondering what's changed your mind about me?'

'I told you, you clean up well.' She seemed to grapple with whatever was on her mind. 'And you brought the boy back in one piece.'

He moved over to the chair and settled himself into its soft cushions.

'Billy's a friend of yours?'

'Him and Charlie both. They're the closest thing I've got to family.' She sighed. 'Charlie's got the good sense to keep away from trouble but Billy, he seems drawn to it.'

'I guess women naturally have more sense than men.' He frowned, recalling Scott's lewd description. 'Why don't you tell me about her?'

'You've spent some time with Billy, there's nothing I can tell you that he won't have already.' She poured herself a cup of coffee. 'That boy worships her. And she's much the same way about him, although she doesn't show it as freely.'

The old woman shook her head thoughtfully. 'Much like you.'

'Me?'

'Yes, you. We've been talking for nigh on half an hour and I don't know anything more about you than I did when you first arrived. There was a time when I could read a man within the first ten minutes of meeting him but you, you don't give anything away.' Again she seemed to struggle with some inner turmoil and when she spoke her voice lacked its former gusto. 'Well, I suppose if you don't kill me in my sleep, you'll come clean when you're ready, but whatever your plans are, I wouldn't spend too much time thinking about them.'

7

Charlie finished her coffee as she watched the tall tow-haired bronc-buster with the black eye and crooked nose lead her horse from the barn. Throwing out the dregs and leaving her cup on the porch step, she met him mid-way across the yard.

'Morning, Al. Thanks for saddling Red.'

He smiled, showing a gap between his front teeth. 'It's the least ah can do for my sweetheart.'

The Texan's voice barely ever rose above a good-natured drawl and it didn't now. Still, she couldn't help glancing back towards the house, to the study window where her uncle spent most of his waking hours. But there was no need to worry. It was early yet, the sun only just clearing the horizon, and it had been a while since

Tom had seen a sunrise.

A couple of cowhands emerged from the bunkhouse and waved before they carried on to the cook shack for breakfast. She waited for them to go inside, although there was no way they could overhear at the distance.

'Don't call me that, someone might hear you.'

'Ah take it you didn't speak to your uncle last night then?'

Charlie wanted to say, yes, that she had told him she was marrying Al the bronc-buster. The only problem was, the conversation had been a little one-sided with him curled up unconscious hugging an empty whiskey bottle to his chest.

'No,' she said, putting the guilt aside. 'Billy went into town last night and it'll be easier to tell Uncle Tom if I have an ally.'

He handed her the reins. 'Sure 'nuff, ah can understand that.'

She wanted to kiss him for being patient. Hold him and forget about the ranch for a while. Enjoy being a woman. But more men were leaving the bunkhouse and with Billy not yet home, the day was already spoiling.

She watched Al follow the other men to the cook shack, waiting until he turned and smiled back at her, then headed out.

Leaving the house in the south meadow with its back-drop of pine-forested mountains, she crossed a small willow-lined creek, then ambled through dense pockets of sweet-smelling Ponderosa pine forest that led out onto grassland and marked the north end of Crooked-W land.

She was still thinking about Al when she saw Billy riding towards her. Eagerly, she waved and heeled Red into a spirited gallop. By the time she reached him, her hat was hanging by its string and her blonde hair had come loose of its single tie.

She had been planning to speak to him about talking to his pa regarding her plans with Al as soon as she saw him, but now she pushed that to the back of her mind.

'Good night?' she asked, noting the slump in his shoulders and the black shadows under his eyes, not to mention the bruise colouring up his cheek. 'Or shouldn't I ask?'

He grinned. 'Well . . . ' he started.

Notwithstanding the pain of his hangover, he then told her about his lucky deuces and the stranger who had made quite an impression on him.

'I told him to come out to the ranch,' he said, 'and there'd be a job for him.'

Billy's voice sounded excited, his pitch high as the two cousins once again rode the length of fence in the north pasture.

'What kind of job?'

'Not sure, although he told me he isn't a cowpuncher.'

It wasn't a straight answer but it told her enough. 'And you're sure he isn't one of Johnson's hired guns?'

Billy nodded. 'I asked him. I said, 'Are you working for Johnson' and he said, 'No', just like that.'

'And of course, if he was working for Johnson, he'd be honest enough to say so.'

'Geez, Charlie, what do you want from me?'

She wanted all the facts, but she had a feeling she wasn't getting them, especially since experience proved that Billy had a habit of only telling her what he wanted her to know.

'I just want you to be careful. All you've told me about this man is that you bought him a drink and he asked a lot of questions, but you don't know the first thing about him, except that he told you he wasn't working for Johnson.' Charlie shrugged. 'With the kind of riff-raff that's been riding into town lately, it's not much to go on.'

Billy's colour had risen and his mouth formed a petulant scowl. Charlie knew there was no point trying to reason with him and as a fresh break in the fence ahead caught her eye, she urged Red forward to put some distance between them while he calmed down.

'Darnit,' she said, as he caught up. 'Twice in two days. And five posts this time. I'm starting to think you're right.'

'I am?'

'Johnson's not going to give up until he gets what he wants.' She felt sick to the pit of her stomach. 'Or somebody stops him.'

Billy laughed. 'Well, yee-ha, welcome back, Rawhide Charlie.'

'Don't, Billy, you know this isn't a game, don't you? Men are going to die. We could die and Johnson could still get the Crooked-W.'

'I know trouble's coming, that's all I know.' He hung his head. 'There's something I didn't tell you about last night . . . '

She held her tongue while he related his run-in with Val Johnson. That he was even there to tell about it was a source of amazement to her. That he had been stupid enough to tell Johnson anything about arrangements at the

Crooked-W beggared belief.

'We should get home, tell your pa what happened,' she said, again noticing the sick feeling in the pit of her stomach. 'If Johnson's coming out here to see him, he can't bury his head in the dirt any longer.'

Billy nodded, his gaze flickering to a point somewhere behind her. 'What the Hell . . . ?'

8

As Charlie turned, a bullet passed her by inches. She glimpsed the shooter a hundred yards away, but with bullets kicking up dirt around them, it was all she could do to keep Red under control. By the time she had pulled the Yellow Boy from its saddle boot, he had mounted up and was riding out of range.

'Come on, we can catch him,' she shouted.

'Charlie!'

The sound of her name, screamed with such anguish, brought her up short. She didn't wait for Red to settle before she flung herself from the saddle. She hit the ground hard, stumbling and landing on her knees with a thud, crawling to reach Billy where he lay crumpled on the ground, clutching his stomach, his breathing ragged, his face contorted with pain.

Her hands shook as she tore at his, needing to know how badly injured he was.

'No,' he screamed. 'Don't touch me.'

'I need to look. I need to know how bad it is.'

He closed his eyes and nodded, but even so, he fought against her when she tried to force his hands away.

'Please, Billy,' she implored, 'you have to let me see.'

At last, she managed to peel away his fingers, but the blood soaking the front of his shirt made it difficult to know where the bullet had entered. Even so, she was sure it was a gut shot.

'It's bad, isn't it?' he managed through a jaw clenched with agony.

She cupped his face, not knowing what to say.

'I feel like my stomach's on fire.'

Despite the panic crushing her, she managed to stay calm. 'I'm going to take you home.'

She tried to pull him up, but his

scream stopped her dead.

He shook his head. 'I'm not going to make it.'

His words were disjointed. Every breath drained more strength out of him, his voice becoming little more than a brittle croak, the words taut and hard won.

'Son-of-a-bitch killed me.'

'You saw who it was?'

'Scott.'

He choked on the word as a fresh spasm made him shudder. However much she wanted it not to be, she knew the end was inevitable.

She tugged his arm, yanking him to his feet despite his cries. 'Get up on that horse because I'm not leaving you.'

* * *

When the ranch house came into view, Charlie kept Red to the steady walk she had maintained since leaving the north pasture. When Al and the ranch foreman came running from the corral, she squeezed Billy's arm.

'Be careful with him. He's hurt real bad.'

Behind him in the saddle, she hung onto him, the way she had as they rode home, until the two men slid him off. As Rand, the foreman, checked on Billy, she saw her uncle hobble out onto the porch. At first he barely glanced in Billy's direction, then the realization hit him that the blood-drenched figure was his son.

He almost buckled. Only the support of his crutches and the porch rail, as he staggered into it, kept him upright. When he looked at Charlie, his expression was blank, disbelieving.

Someone tugged her arm. Caught her when she fell. Sat her down. Shoved something between her lips. And then a cool shot of water hit her at the back of the throat. She coughed, spluttered, panic jolting her back to reality.

'Billy?'

She couldn't see him. Legs, backs, bodies blocked her view.

'What happened?' Tom asked. 'Who did this?'

She shook her head, at a loss as to what to tell him, her mind a jumble of facts and accusations. The long ride home, blaming herself, reassuring Billy that everything would be all right, wondering if things might have been different if —

'Where were you?' Tom asked.

'Up in the north pasture.' She could barely get the words out, her breath coming in short bursts, but she was determined. 'Somebody pulled down part of the fence. We were about to head back when *bang*.'

'Did you see who it was?'

When she didn't answer, Tom looked to Rand who was closing Billy's bloody shirt.

'How bad is it?' he asked.

Rand's face was grey, his eyes damp and misty when he looked up. 'He's gone.'

She could see him now the men were moving away. His face was grey, his lips were blue, his skin, she knew, was already cold.

'Who did this, Charlie? Who killed my son?'

'Scott,' she mumbled.

'Scott Johnson? You're sure? You saw him? It was definitely him?'

For the first time in a long while, Charlie sensed urgency in her uncle and latched onto it. 'Billy said Scott Johnson threatened him, told him to watch his back. I'd bet my horse, he's the one who did this.'

As usual Tom's tone fell to a drone. 'So you didn't see him?'

'Billy said . . . ' She nodded, convincing herself. 'It was him. He murdered Billy. Johnson's fired the first shot.'

'Whoa, let's not start throwing accusations around.'

'Then when? He's murdered Billy. We can't just stand around and wait for him to roll right over us,' she said, choking on the words her cousin had used.

'What are you talking about, roll right over us?'

For a second, she stared at her uncle. Short and blunt in stature, his black hair run through with grey, his brown eyes dull and his shoulders rounded like the weight of the world had sat on them his whole life, he presented a picture of defeat.

'You really don't see it, do you?'

It sounded more like an accusation than a question.

'See what? That my son is dead? You think I don't see that?'

'That Johnson is taking over this country. He already owns most of the town and now he's got his sights set on the Crooked-W. This is the start.'

He waved her accusations away. 'Johnson's not going to bother us. We've got an agreement.'

'What kind of agreement?'

'An agreement between two businessmen.'

In spite of her uncle's condescending tone, it was his apparent lack of understanding that dumbfounded her and served to fuel her growing frustration.

'Businessman? He's a goddamn outlaw!'

Tom shifted on his crutches, irritation starting to mask the shock of losing his son. 'Watch your language, Charlie. He served his time and now he's trying to make a go of it, just like the rest of us. I would have expected you, of all people, to at least give him the benefit of the doubt.'

'Me, of all people?' She huffed. 'That's rich coming from you.'

'That's enough. I won't have you take that tone with me.'

Dismissing her with a turn of his shoulder, her uncle looked amongst the faces of the men gathered to witness the commotion. They shifted restlessly. To most of them Charlie was the unofficial lady boss, their orders and their pay came through her. She had hired most of them.

'Al,' Tom said, pointing him out.

'Ride into town and fetch the marshal.'

'The marshal?' Quick as a cat, Charlie jumped to her feet. 'Why?'

'He's the law.'

'The law? He's the law for Val Johnson. You need to deal with this, not leave it to some hired gun with a badge.'

He shook his head stubbornly. 'The law's the law. Once we ignore it, how are we any better than the law-breakers?'

'Is that what this is about? Making sure you don't get tarred with the same brush as — '

'Enough!'

This time his voice carried like the crack of a whip, but Charlie was too incensed to stop. 'You're going to get us all killed. Billy was right. We need to make a stand, fight for what's ours. Don't you see that?'

A couple of the men nodded. She might be a woman, but she had strength of character that her uncle lacked, and more often these days the men were listening to what she had to say. Even Rand, her uncle's friend of twenty years, seemed reluctant to meet his gaze.

Charlie felt hopeful expectation welling up inside her as she watched her uncle's expression harden and his knuckles turn white where he gripped the crutches. She could almost see him shake with anger, but when he spoke his voice was low and calm.

'All I see is a girl overcome with grief, looking for someone to blame. But instead of blaming me, why don't you ask yourself why Billy's really dead? I warned you to stay away from that boundary fence. Maybe if you had, Billy would still be alive.'

If he had slapped her across the face, she couldn't have been more stunned.

Al grabbed her around the waist and clamped his hand over her mouth as she shouted. She wasn't even sure what she had said but the damage was clearly done. The crutch tip slammed into her shoulder with the power of a kicking horse and she felt Al stagger as the force knocked them both backwards.

'I won't have you speak to me that way, Charlie.'

Tom applied varying degrees of pressure as he punctuated each word. Her shoulder throbbed where the tip of the crutch continued to dig in just below the collar-bone.

'You'll apologize to me, right now.'

Stubbornly, she pressed her lips into a tight line. Maybe she had gone too far but she wasn't ready to back down, even though convention said she should. At last she had done what Billy had wanted from the start, and if she had found the strength to speak out sooner, he might still be alive. As much as Billy's death was her uncle's fault, it was hers too.

After a painfully long silence, Tom dropped the crutch back to its usual position under his right arm. 'You better get out of my sight, girl, until you learn some respect.'

She started to retort but decided

against it. With her heart racing and the blood pounding in her ears loud enough to deafen her, she had to admit she probably wasn't thinking straight. Not to mention it wasn't right arguing when Billy lay cold and dead on the ground not five feet away. Mostly, she held her silence because her uncle was a fool and no good ever came from arguing with a fool.

Breaking free of Al's grip, she pushed through the group of men and mounted up.

'Charlie.' It was Al. He placed his big bony hand on her knee. 'Now wait just a minute and ah'll come with you.'

She shook her head.

'Ah'm not lettin' you go anywhere on your own with a killer on the loose.'

'He's long gone. If he wanted to kill me he could have done it anywhere on the ride back here. Please, Al, I just need some time on my own. I won't go far.' She leaned down and kissed him on the cheek. 'I promise.'

He nodded, although he looked none

too happy about it. ‘All right, but don’t go into town and if you’re not here when ah get back from fetchin’ the marshal, ah’m comin’ to find you.’

9

Sunrise. The dawning of a new day. The chance to wipe old slates clean and start afresh. Usually, it was one of Charlie's favourite times, but as she finished saddling Red the next morning, she didn't feel her usual optimism. This wasn't the first time she had spent the night under a blanket of stars, but it felt like the longest.

Leaving the horse to chew grass, she dropped down in her favourite spot and pulled her knees up to her chin. It would be a few minutes until the sun started its ascent. Until then, the grey sky seemed to mimic her mood and although her gaze fixed on the far horizon, waiting for the first glow across the distant mountaintops, she couldn't stop her mind from wandering.

After crying herself dry over Billy, she had gone to sleep seething and woken up remorseful, yet still stead-fast in her belief that a line had been crossed. She didn't believe her uncle disagreed. What separated them was her conviction that they should be doing something as opposed to his belief that the law should be allowed to prevail.

Law. Pah!

Already this month a dozen known outlaws, mostly gunmen, had joined Johnson. On any given day she could ride into town and see two horses she didn't recognize. Barely any decent folk ventured onto the street after 2 o'clock in the afternoon.

As she waited for the first glimpse of sunrise over the mountains, she noticed she was trembling. It didn't take a fool to see that she was hurting over Billy, not thinking straight. In the heat of the moment, she had strapped on her gun, but what purpose would that serve now? She couldn't save Billy. She hadn't saved him when it counted.

At last the rising sun cast a rosy glow across the sky, spreading amber rays over the mountains to stretch tentatively across the valley floor. Charlie swiped at the tears trickling down her cheeks as she thought about Billy. No matter how hard she tried, it was impossible not to take some of the blame for what had happened to him.

It was the distant echo of gunfire that interrupted her thoughts. For a second it sounded like a distant clap of thunder, causing her to stop and puzzle it. But there was no storm in the sky and realization and foreboding launched her onto her feet and into the saddle.

By the time she crested the ridge overlooking the ranch buildings, the house was already ablaze, the yard strewn with bodies. She almost rode headlong into the carnage but at the last second she pulled back into a stand of cottonwoods. Yanking on the reins she barely waited for the red horse to slow down before she slid from the saddle. From her position, laid low on the ridge overlooking the yard, she tried to find her uncle among the figures running around but there were no faces she recognized, only Val Johnson. With his head held high, Johnson seemed impervious to the chaos around him. The smoke and the heat and the flying embers seemed to neither affect nor worry him, the latter demanding no more than an absent-minded swat when any dared land on him.

It seemed to Charlie that Hell recognized one of its own.

She continued to watch as he beckoned to two men and pointed them towards a figure lying on the ground. After a short exchange, they picked up the man and carried him towards the house. Charlie stifled a cry and held onto it, watching as the men swung the body into the burning structure just seconds before the roof caved in. Before she could pull her collar across her face, a cloud of choking smoke billowed towards her, blocking out the sun

Pressing herself closer to the ground, she tried to stifle the gagging cough that started in the back of her throat then seemed to claw its way from her lungs. When she dared look up again through painful, teary eyes, Johnson was speaking to another man, gesturing at the surrounding area. When they were finished, the man mounted a nearby horse and rode away, heading towards the ridge.

Suddenly it dawned on her. They were looking for her.

Keeping low to the ground, she stumbled back to Red.

10

'Daniel.'

Light pressure on his arm brought him fully awake. As his eyes adjusted to the dim light from the hallway, he recognized Ma standing over him.

'What is it?'

'Get dressed,' she whispered. 'Meet me in the kitchen.'

Although he had no idea what had provoked the impromptu wake-up call, he decided to strap on his gun. After checking it was loaded, he headed downstairs carrying his hat and coat in his left hand.

Standing in the kitchen doorway, looking almost grey with worry, Ma handed him a cup of coffee and waved him towards the chair by the fire.

'I'm sorry I busted in on you, but I'm worried,' she said before he could ask. 'I saw Johnson and that boy of his ride out with some of his men earlier. It ain't usual for them to be up and out this early and it's got me worried.'

'What are you thinking?'

'They're up to no good. Now I know you haven't been straight with me since you got here, and I'm sure you've got your reasons for that, but I'd be mighty obliged if you'd take a ride out to the Crooked-W and take a look around for me.'

'What do you think I'm going to find?'

She didn't seem to be listening as she peered out through the window. 'Just a look, mind you, because — oh, my Lord!'

Daniel's hand reached automatically for his gun, his senses on alert. Daylight filtered in where the curtains had been pushed back and Ma stood on tiptoes with her face almost pressed against the glass.

The large window offered a good view of the open grassland behind the hotel and Daniel's gaze followed hers.

He saw a chestnut mare carrying a rider wearing a long duster over chaps and jeans, and an old Stetson that shadowed his face. A rope looped around the saddle and a rifle in the boot suggested he was probably a cowhand.

But it didn't explain why the old woman seemed so upset.

His hand hovered over his gun. 'Ma, is everything all right?'

She turned, gesturing for him to take the chair by the fire, a finger pressed to her lips warning him to stay silent before she dragged the newcomer inside, slammed the door and pulled the curtains together. Finally, she pulled out a bench and manoeuvred the newcomer onto it.

'What in Lord's name are you doing here?' Impatiently, she swept off the hat. 'Where's Billy? What happened? What is this? Soot?'

Daniel's breath caught not only at the acrid stench of smoke that had followed the girl in but also at the sight she presented. About as tall as him, at five-nine, she didn't carry an ounce of fat and her face, although dirty and tearstained, carried a deep tan against her long sun-bleached hair.

'Scott killed Billy and then his pa and his outlaw crew killed Uncle Tom. They killed everybody.'

'Lord, no.' The old woman almost sank to her knees but caught hold of the table and leaned against it for support. 'Tell me what happened.'

The girl glanced towards Daniel. 'Who's he?'

'His name's Daniel, don't worry about him. He won't be any trouble.' Ma leaned in close. 'Although whether he'll turn out to be any help, I don't know.'

Daniel smarted at the remark but he knew he deserved it. She'd given him every opportunity to come clean and still he hadn't told her who he was or why he was there.

Turning the girl away from him, Ma encouraged her to go on.

'Scott killed Billy and I argued with

Uncle Tom. I spent the night on Molly's Mount. This morning I heard gunshots and I rode back to the ranch and they were all dead. He killed Uncle Tom and threw his body in the flames.' The words had flowed out without nary a breath but now she choked. 'Nobody stood a chance. They just killed everybody and then burned the place down. The Crooked-W's gone. Billy's dead. Uncle Tom's dead. Al's dead.'

Ma wiped the girl's face with a cloth. 'Billy? Tom? Dead? How did you manage to get away?'

'When I got back, they didn't see me. When I came up on the ridge they were shooting anybody who was still alive. It was an execution. After I saw what they did to Uncle Tom . . . I knew there was nothing I could do and then I saw them start looking for me.'

The girl's voice cracked with emotion but somehow she held herself together. 'He's going to kill me. He's going to find me and kill me.'

Ma seemed genuinely horrified. 'No,

that won't happen. I won't let it.'

'You can't stop them. After what they've done they can't leave any witnesses. I shouldn't have come here. I shouldn't be here. I've put you in danger. I need to get away, far away.'

The girl was suddenly hysterical and Ma was struggling to keep her seated. Daniel was half up when Ma gave her a hard shake. It seemed to do the trick.

'You're not going anywhere so just settle down.'

The words seemed to be for both of them and Daniel sat back. For a full minute, nothing disturbed the peace. Twisting her apron in her hands, Ma was clearly unsure what to say or do. At last, she shook her head and walked away. After a few minutes of banging and clattering, she brought a cup of coffee. She offered it to the girl, clasping her hands and the cup between her own as the girl shook uncontrollably.

'There's only one place you can go and one person who can keep you safe, if you can find your way back there.' She shot a thoughtful glance in Daniel's direction. 'Your pa.'

'My pa?' The girl almost dropped the coffee. 'He's been dead for ten years.'

'Take my word for it, he was alive and well the last I heard.'

'But you all told me he was dead.'

'That was your Uncle Tom's idea, to stop you trying to run away. I begged him not to. It wasn't right, but he thought it was for the best.' Ma placed a hand on her shoulder and Daniel saw a tear on the old woman's cheek. 'I send your pa word every year, tell him how you are. If he was dead, I'd know.'

'You lied to me all this time?' Her voice had risen to a crescendo but now it dropped to barely a whisper. 'How could you?'

'Please, Charlie, you know anything I did was out of concern for you.' She tried to stroke her hair but Charlie slapped her hand away. 'Well at least stay and finish your coffee. I'll put some supplies together, get you some clean clothes to change into and be back in a couple of minutes when you've had time to think about it.'

The old woman scurried away.

Again Charlie looked across to Daniel. 'You're Daniel Smith?'

'Call me Daniel.'

'Billy told me he talked to you. He said you weren't working for Johnson. Are you?'

'No.'

She sipped at her drink then pushed it away and stared at the door. Caught up in her thoughts, she didn't hear him move until he was standing right behind her. Her surprise made them both start and he grabbed her elbow to steady her.

'I didn't mean to scare you.'

'I don't scare that easy.'

The way she looked him square in the eye didn't contradict the boast but, whether she was aware of it or not, she was shaking.

'I need to tell you something,' he said, but before he could say more,

Ma rejoined them, her head turned quizzically towards the sound of an approaching rider.

'Stay here.' Rushing outside, she slammed the door before either of them could argue.

Seconds later, she shouted, 'Scott Johnson. What do you want?'

'Where is she?' The rider's tone matched hers for animosity. 'I know that's her horse standing there, old woman. Where's she hiding?'

'She ain't hiding from the likes of you.'

The sound of a scuffle, the thud of a blow, was followed by a shriek of pain.

'Come out, Charlie, or I'll shoot the old woman. You know I'll do it.'

Despite the coffee he had drunk, Daniel's mouth was already dry with foreboding. When Charlie got to her feet, he tried to stop her, but she shrugged him off.

'Stay out of it,' she warned.

He let her go, hanging back. Time would tell if she needed his help and, if she did, the element of surprise wouldn't hurt.

'Stop that,' she shouted, striding forward to stand between Ma and the rider before his horse trampled her underfoot. 'You lay another hand on her and I swear it'll be the last thing you ever do.'

11

Without really thinking, Charlie had gone outside with all the confidence of a cattle baron, but inside, she felt more like a steer about to go under the branding iron. She sensed more than heard movement behind her but taking her eyes off Scott now would be like turning her back on a mad dog. Besides, if the man inside had lied and was working for Johnson, seeing him come for her wouldn't make any difference, especially with her gun still in its holster. She cursed herself for that mistake.

With legs threatening to buckle, she walked further out into the yard, close enough to show she wasn't afraid, which was about as far from the truth as you could get, yet far enough away that she didn't have to bend her neck to look up at him.

'Still acting all high and mighty, I see,' Scott said.

Just seeing him made her want to throw a punch, but he had at least a head-height and fifty pounds on her, not to mention a reputation for being a mean son-of-a-bitch. With the sun rising behind him, and her eyes still smarting from the smoke, she couldn't make out his features but luckily for her, she guessed he was finding the situation more amusing than threatening.

'I didn't touch the old woman. She ran out, frightened the horse and got kicked.'

Charlie glanced down at Ma, crumpled on the ground with a wizened hand pressed against her forehead. 'Do you expect me to believe that?'

Scott shrugged without a hint of remorse as he removed his leather gloves and tucked them in his coat pocket before dismounting. As he closed the gap between them, his spurs jingled, marking each slow deliberate stride until he stopped just a step away from her.

Still she held her ground, until he tilted his hat back to reveal more clearly his sooty face.

'You look like you just saw a ghost,' he said, grinning when she took a step away. 'I guess I get more handsome every time you see me.'

Standing there wearing a blue shirt and jeans, he reminded her of the boy he had been the first time she met him, before she knew who he was. But although he was undeniably handsome, his wide smile fell short of the green eyes that lacked any hint of warmth.

'All right then, let's cut the chitchat. Get on your horse. My pa wants to talk to you.' When she didn't move, he grabbed her arm. 'It wasn't a request.'

Despite the blood trickling from her forehead, Ma tried to stand but only managed to get to her knees before a shove from Scott sent her rolling helplessly in the dirt.

Charlie lunged, while his guard was

down, pushing hard enough to stagger him but not enough to get the upper hand. She threw herself into him again. This time, he grabbed her, struggling to get his arms around her as a tumult of emotion added momentum to the spirited fight she was putting up.

'Stop that, you crazy Hellcat,' he ordered, getting her under control.

Wrapped in a bear hug and powerless against his greater strength, Charlie quietened down. Scott loosened his hold, as she knew he would.

'That's better. Now — '

Bringing her knee up, she aimed for his groin, but he was quick and instead the movement glanced off his inner thigh. She smelled tobacco on his breath as he pulled her in tight against his body, stifling any further fight she might put up.

'I ain't in the mood for games. You and me have got business to take care of and you can either ride in the saddle or over it.'

Loosening his grip, he shoved her

towards Red, and when she made a break he barely caught the arm of her coat. Pulled off balance, she reeled backwards and collided with him and it looked like they were both heading for a fall. Somehow Scott kept his footing, but the effort was too much for his temper and he lashed out, catching her a hard blow across the cheek.

'Damn it, girl, why do you have to do things the hard way?' This time, he grabbed her arm in a white-knuckle grip that made her wince with pain. 'I warned you. If you won't come of your own free will, then you're going to have to be tied.' He reached his free hand into his coat pocket and pulled out a length of cord. 'Hold still!'

A shot startled them all.

'I think the lady's made it clear she doesn't want to go with you. So let her go.'

Peering towards the door, Charlie held her breath on a surge of relief. Daniel was leaning casually against the frame, his gun back in its holster, his thumbs resting on his shell belt. The fall of his hair shadowed his face but his tone had brooked no argument.

Scott pulled Charlie in tighter against him. 'This is none of your business, mister.'

'When you beat an old woman and tried to kidnap the lady, you made it my business.'

'Is that so? Who's your friend, Charlie?' Scott asked without taking his stare away from the newcomer.

She hesitated, her gaze taking in the dusty but passable clothes, pausing briefly on the gun holstered at his hip. She remembered seeing a grey horse, a worn half-seat saddle in the lean-to. Nothing about him gave her much of a clue as to his character.

'Does it matter?' Daniel asked. 'I still want you to let her go.'

'And I want you to turn around and go back inside. This doesn't concern you, cowpoke.'

It was a deliberate insult and maybe would have offended someone else, but

Daniel just smiled.

'You see now that's where we disagree.'

'Is that so? In that case, do you know how to handle that gun you're wearing?'

'Well enough.'

It wasn't a definitive answer and Charlie felt Scott tense, his breathing quicken against her hair. After a few seconds, he shoved her aside.

'Do you know who I am?' He flicked the edge of his coat back to reveal the .38 Smith & Wesson in a holster tied against his thigh.

Charlie felt inevitability drop in the pit of her stomach like a blacksmith's hammer on an anvil, leaving her feeling sick to her boots. Carefully, she started to back away.

'Stay where you are,' Scott ordered.

She stopped.

'I know who you are and I don't care, but maybe you should be wondering who I am if you're going to pick a fight,' Daniel countered, walking out into the open. 'Then again, I guess it makes no difference really. All you need to know is that where I come from women are treated with respect.'

'Seems to me like you need to learn some of that yourself, cowpoke.'

'I've got respect, but not for scum who'd tie up a woman and throw her over a horse like a sack of flour. Make your move whenever you're ready.'

Scott moseyed forward and Daniel let him come, his body relaxed, his face impassive. When the punch came, he reacted like a coiled spring, blocking and sidestepping in one movement, but Scott was quick and swept his foot out from under him. He tried to take Scott down with him but Scott was no slouch. He avoided the tackle and, almost like a well-practised dance, spun and kicked, narrowly missing Daniel's face and instead leaving a bloody slash where his spur raked a defensive arm. A couple of fierce kicks to the ribs and stomach left Daniel doubled up and gasping, but as he braced for more,

Scott backed off.

'Not as tough as you thought, are you, cowpoke?' Excitement made Scott's words come high and fast like a young girl's. 'Remember that the next time you stick your nose into other people's business.'

He grabbed Charlie's wrist, dragging her in close and wrapping his arm around her waist. Dropping his voice lower, he spoke against her ear.

'Unless you want me to finish what I've started with your friend there, climb on your horse and don't give me any more trouble.'

Tears filled her eyes but she held them back. Scott might have the upper hand but she'd be damned if she'd let him see her cry.

Daniel pulled himself onto his hands and knees and spat blood. 'Don't go with him on my account. I'm just getting warmed up.'

Charlie shook her head. 'There's been enough killing today.'

Scott laughed. 'She's right. There has

been a lot.' He turned his attention to Daniel. 'But one more cowpoke won't hurt.'

12

Daniel wasn't even fully on his feet when the shot came. Instinctively, he dived to the side, expecting at any moment to feel the explosion of pain that would mark his death. Luckily for him, as Scott pushed Charlie aside and fired, his shot went wide, splintering the water trough. From hours of practice, Daniel's palm hit the walnut grip of his Smith & Wesson and the weapon jumped into his hand.

For a split second, he wondered whether to give him a chance. After all, killing him would break a promise Daniel had made to his ma on her deathbed, not to mention being a waste of a good bullet. On the other hand, Scott was a loudmouth with a gun and an attitude, a bee drawn to honey.

In the end, Daniel hardly felt the trigger move under his finger.

Blood flared on the red head's sleeve, his pistol falling to the ground as he grabbed his shoulder and reeled on legs suddenly too weak to hold him.

'Son of a bitch!' he shouted.

Daniel covered the ground between them in a run, kicking the gun aside before Scott could fully regain his wits.

'I'm the sonofabitch, says the man who draws on another man when he's on his knees,' he yelled.

Even backed into a corner, looking into the barrel of a .38, Scott's arrogant expression challenged him. Daniel felt sorely tempted to pull the trigger again, even if only to inflict another painful wound, but he wouldn't in front of Charlie. Even though his finger itched to prove a point.

'That's enough.'

The sound of a rifle being readied for action stopped them all dead in their tracks.

Common sense told Daniel he should keep his own counsel, but seeing the steady way Charlie held the Yellow

Boy made him stay his hand. He slipped the gun into its holster and hooked his thumbs in his shell belt, waiting to see what would happen.

It came as no surprise when Scott piped up. 'You wouldn't shoot me. That's not the way your yellow uncle raised you, is it?'

'Watch your mouth,' Daniel growled, 'or I'll shoot you in the other arm.'

'I appreciate the offer,' Charlie said, 'but please let me handle this.'

Daniel nodded, although he wasn't happy about it.

Her eyes narrowed but she kept her ire in check. 'Ma, would you pick up Scott's gun and throw it in the water trough? I wouldn't like him to get any ideas that might get one of us killed.'

Without hesitation, the old woman did as she was bid, the gun making a loud splash and startling the horses when it hit the water and sank with a plug. Scott's eyes shone with the desire to kill, as he grinned boyishly. 'It ain't an idea, Charlie. It's always been the plan. I was just hoping you and me could have some fun first.'

'Watch your mouth.'

'Or what? You're going to shoot me? You haven't got the guts.' Scott's laughter made a nasty hollow sound. 'You won't shoot me. You're weak like the rest of your family. Billy saw it coming and never even moved. And your uncle, he just stood there and waited for it, like a bottle on a wall, and my pa gave it to him.'

Colour flooded Charlie's cheeks, her features twisting into a mask of unguarded hatred as she moved in on him, stopping dangerously close. When she eventually spoke, her words were low and cold.

'I should kill you but I won't, not because I'm yellow but because, if I did, I'd be no better than you. And I am better than you. And one day, you'll get yours and I'll be there to see it and I'll know I was better than you.'

'The only thing I'm going to get is the Crooked-W, but you won't be around to see it.'

'You'll never get your hands on the Crooked-W.'

'Who's going to stop me? You? You might dress like a man, ride like a man, but you're still just a silly woman. What can a woman do against the might of a man?'

Scott tried to lunge but, in the same instant, Charlie swung the stock of the rifle at his head. The crack sounded like a shot and Scott went down. Another couple of anger-fuelled blows laid him out cold.

Charlie stepped back, her breathing laboured. Ambling forward to peer at Scott lying limp and silent in a puddle of blood, Ma kicked his leg. 'He's still . . . alive.' She sounded disappointed. 'You should have shot him.'

Charlie turned away and heaved.

'No, she shouldn't.'

Ma shifted her attention. 'Then why didn't you, Daniel Cliff?'

13

'Don't look so surprised. You're a dead ringer for your pa. Did you really think I wouldn't recognize you? And Smith, what kind of fool alias is that?'

'It seemed like a good idea at the time. I wasn't sure you'd want to see me.'

She shook her head. 'You're my sister's boy, why wouldn't I?'

'Because I know my ma wrote to you. You know I wasn't always a credit to her.'

'I still don't see why it was necessary to lie to me,' Ma grumbled. 'But none of that's important now. Let's go inside.'

As they filed back into the kitchen, no one cast a glance in Scott's direction. The blood seeping from a gash in his scalp was already drying under the heat of a fast-rising sun and it was unlikely he'd wake up for hours after the beating Charlie had given him.

Within minutes Ma had everyone organized and while Charlie sat quietly gripping a cup of coffee, Daniel stripped off his shirt and allowed the old woman to assess his wounds.

'I'm guessing he bruised a couple of ribs,' she said, making him wince as she prodded. 'Still, it could have been worse.'

'If he had killed me, you mean?'

'If he had taken Charlie. They were no idle threats he was making before she bashed his head in. They'll want her dead nearly as much as they want . . . whatever else it is they want.'

Daniel watched Charlie for a minute while he supped his coffee. She hadn't said a word and he wondered if maybe now the imminent danger had passed she was in shock. It was impossible to know what thoughts were going through her mind while she stared at the rifle on the table in front of her, but Daniel guessed it wouldn't be anything good.

Ma finished prodding his ribs and moved on to the slash on his forearm. 'It's deep but I don't have time to stitch it. The sooner you're on your way the better. Random shots are nothing new in this town but you never know, somebody might get nosy.'

'Still trying to get rid of me.'

Ma rubbed some evil-smelling salve into the wound. It smarted, but he thought better than to ask what it was.

'Your ma hoped I'd be able to talk some sense into you, you know, keep you out of trouble.' She grunted. 'It's obvious to a blind man that ain't going to happen now. So, the way I see it, you may as well put your reputation to good use.'

'I've got a reputation?'

Ma scowled. 'Your ma said you were angling for one. Although, the beating Scott gave you makes me wonder what kind of reputation it is you're hoping for.' She glanced across at Charlie. 'But what other choice do we have?'

Daniel's arm throbbed as she bandaged it tightly, all the while muttering. Finally, she rummaged in a cupboard and brought out a coarse grey work shirt. She measured it up against him.

'It'll have to do. Get dressed, there's no time to waste.'

There didn't seem much point in arguing, not over a shirt at least, and gingerly he worked his way into it. Apart from being a little tight across the shoulders and generous everywhere else, it did the job.

'Care to tell me what your plan is?'

She glared at him as though she had already given him the details and resented having to repeat them.

'I like the way you stood between Charlie and that no-good cur Scott. It showed strength of character. Whatever happens next, she's going to need someone looking out for her.'

'And you think I'm the one to do that?'

'That's what I'm saying, ain't it?

You're not very quick on the uptake, are you, so I'll spell it out. Once Scott regains his senses, he'll be gunning for you. I'm betting on you not wanting to die and being as handy with that iron as your ma said you are. If you're not . . . ' She threw up her hands. 'I don't know.'

'Or I could just mind my own business and ride back the way I came,' he said, his ire rising.

He almost flinched under the withering look she gave him.

'I wouldn't blame you if you did, Mr . . . Daniel.' Charlie picked up the Yellow Boy and walked across to join them. 'But Ma's right. I'm going to need help. If she's prepared to trust you, then I guess I'll have to.'

Although the coffee had brought some colour back to her cheeks, her shoulders were slumped and she still looked shaky.

'But I don't know you and you don't know me.' She looked him squarely in the eye. 'Just know that I'm grateful for the way you stepped in to help me but if you want to walk away, I'll understand. If, on the other hand, you want to earn twenty dollars a day . . . '

'My gun's not for hire if that's what you're asking.'

'I wouldn't hire you if it was. I don't need that kind of man watching my back,' she said, pausing only slightly, probably to question her sanity, 'but that's not to say I might not make the offer later . . . if there is a later. The fact is, on my own, I'm no match for Scott or the kind of men Val Johnson will send after me. All I'm asking is that you help me get to my pa. Be an extra pair of eyes. Cover my back. It's a two-day ride — '

'Probably nearer to three,' Ma cut in.

'A three-day ride then. If we survive, maybe I'll have a chance of getting some justice for Billy and my uncle and Al and all those other men that died today.'

Daniel didn't need to think about it. This was the reason he had come to Ranch Town, to meet this girl and find out what she knew about the location of the Wells gang's hideout. Now she was offering more than he could have hoped for: safe passage in.

14

Even as they rode away, Charlie wondered if she wouldn't be better making the trip alone. After all, she was used to long days in the saddle, and Red seemed eager to be away when she turned his head south. But what of Daniel Cliff? Although he had made light of his injuries, Charlie had once bruised her ribs after a run-in with a goat and she knew how painful it could be. Would he be more of a hindrance than a help if it came to a fight?

They rode in silence with Charlie always in the lead, but each of them watching their back trail. Around midday they stopped to rest the horses then they pressed on again. Across the prairie, nothing stirred the hot air. The sun was hanging low in the sky by the time they reached the foothills.

Charlie drew Red to a stop, seeming

undecided on their direction as her gaze scoured the hills and the mountains beyond.

'Why are we stopping?' Daniel asked.

'Because if you want to change your mind about riding with me, this is your last chance.'

He hid the slight offence the question caused. After all, they had been thrown together out of necessity without the benefit of introduction. She had seen him take a beating, and any fool could do that. What else would she think? And what would she think if she knew his real reason for coming along?

'I've got no intention of leaving you out here on your own,' he said.

'And I appreciate that, but you're not from around these parts. Maybe you don't know where we're headed.'

He knew all right. Fifteen years before, the Wells gang had set up their headquarters somewhere in the mountains beyond these hills. In all that time no one had ever disclosed the exact location, although the area regularly attracted outlaws hopeful of outrunning the law or throwing in their lot with a gang that had made a success out of robbing banks and trains.

'I know we're heading into outlaw territory.'

'That doesn't bother you?'

The truth was, it couldn't have worked out better, but for now he would keep his motives to himself.

'You don't strike me as the kind of woman who would ride into the mountains unless she had a pretty good plan.'

She smiled, the small quirk of her mouth relieving the tension that had etched itself into tired lines across her face. 'I'm not so sure about that, but as long as you're prepared to do what I do, follow my lead, we should be all right.'

For the next couple of hours, they climbed steadily through scrub oak and pines towards the flat rim. Now halfway up, Charlie noticed the sky was quickly darkening.

Drawing to a stop, she took a swig from her canteen, watching Daniel as he reached carefully for his. He hadn't uttered one word of complaint but his pale complexion and drawn expression showed that his injuries and her relentless pace were taking a toll on him.

'We'll bed down here for the night,' she said. 'We've got a lot of riding to do and the horses will be grateful for the rest.'

Leaving Red, she walked around the area, finally settling on a spot sheltered behind two natural slabs each at least eight feet high. With luck they would offer enough cover to allow a small fire that should go unseen if they were being followed. Not to mention that the view across the terrain behind them was unhindered for miles and they would see anyone approaching long before they themselves were discovered.

'This looks like a good place to me.'

Daniel glanced around and nodded before climbing slowly down from the saddle. He didn't complain but he looked all in.

'I'll see to the horses.' Charlie gathered the reins for both animals and started leading them away before he could argue. 'Why don't you get a fire started and get some coffee going.'

Later, with the animals settled and a meal of ham and Ma's biscuits settling in her stomach, Charlie leaned back against her saddle, staring into the dying embers of the fire. When she glanced across at Daniel his eyes were closed, his chin sagging on his chest, his empty cup hanging from his hand where it rested on his thigh.

Again, she wondered whether bringing him along had been the right decision.

'Are you awake?' she asked.

His eyes opened to meet her gaze. 'Do you want me to take the first watch?'

'No, I was thinking about your arm. I should take a look at it.'

Getting to her feet, she circled the

fire and knelt beside him. 'Do you have those supplies Ma gave you?'

He pointed to his saddle-bags lying on the ground nearby. 'Help yourself.'

By the time she retrieved the salve and several lengths of bandage, he had his sleeve rolled up and was fiddling with the small knot Ma had used to finish off her handiwork. A patch of blood showed on the bindings.

Deftly, Charlie pulled a five-inch double-edged knife from a sheath inside her boot. 'Let me.'

She cut the closure, slid the knife back home and unwound the sticky material. He winced as she peeled away the bandages from the puckered skin and winced again when she bathed the wound with water. The edges of the four-inch gash were red, and gaped when she applied pressure.

'It needs stitching.'

'Have you got a needle and thread hidden in your other boot, by any chance?'

Despite his obvious discomfort, there

was a hint of humour in his voice and despite the heaviness of her mood, she found herself reciprocating.

'No, but if I tell you I never sewed a button on a shirt that didn't fall off, you might see that as a blessing.'

After she had finished ministering to his wounds, they finished off the coffee. Neither one seemed eager to talk, but after a while the silence crowded in on Charlie, bringing with it unfamiliar feelings of doubt and fear.

'Are you wondering if I'll be all right in a fight?' Daniel asked, as if reading her mind. He chuckled when she didn't answer. 'It'd be a fair question, one you maybe should have asked before you brought me along.'

'Hindsight is a wonderful thing. Maybe you're asking yourself the same question.' She pondered for a moment. 'It's not every man that likes taking orders from a woman.'

'I was brought up by a strong woman. Taking orders from another one doesn't bother me.'

It was a good answer. Reassuring in a way.

'You should get some rest,' she said. 'We've got a lot of riding ahead of us tomorrow.'

'What about you? Don't you need to sleep?'

With her mind relentlessly replaying the events of the day, she knew sleep would be elusive.

* * *

It was a few hours before dawn when Charlie decided to rouse him. Although he had fallen asleep like a man shot dead, she couldn't rest. Her mind refused to stop its perpetual torment with tiredness only adding emotion to her already tortured thoughts. She had been pacing but as soon as she approached him Daniel's eyes opened.

'I'll wake you when it starts to get light,' he said, without waiting to be asked.

As he pushed off the blanket, she

noticed the gun resting against his thigh. When he had removed it from the holster, she couldn't say, but she felt herself relax knowing that he had.

15

As a pale dawn broke along the horizon, Daniel glanced in Charlie's direction. Although during a fitful sleep she had thrown off the blanket, her grip on the Yellow Boy never slackened. It worried him some as she fretted in her dreams. But not as much as the movement that caught his eye out on the prairie.

He saddled the horses before he woke her. Then, whispering her name, he touched her arm lightly, waiting as she blinked the sleep from her red-rimmed eyes before beckoning her to a place behind one of the two tall slabs where they could see the prairie.

'There.' He pointed away into the distance. 'Do you see that fire? If they're Johnson's men, they must have left not long after we did and made camp when they lost the light to track us.'

'Out in the open like that?'

'Why not? If they think you're alone, they won't be worried about you seeing them. Ma won't have told them anything and Scott doesn't know enough about me to be concerned.'

She put her face in her hands and sighed.

'We've got a head start at least,' Daniel said. 'And coming up this hill will slow them down. Their horses are going to need to rest a while once they reach the top. We should be able to stay ahead of them but it won't be for long.'

After a few seconds, she raised her head. 'Maybe we should make a stand here. Two of them, two of us. It sounds like a fair fight, especially since we've got the high ground.'

Her reasoning didn't surprise him. In the short time he had known her, she had tackled every obstacle head on, from standing up to Scott to putting her trust in a stranger. But by her own admission, her judgement could be flawed. And on this occasion, he thought it was.

'Knowing where we are, do you really think that improves our chances?'

Indecision showed in the pinched set of her mouth, but there was no sign of stubbornness or challenge when she asked, 'What do you think we should do?'

He gave it some final consideration. 'Try to put some more distance between them and us. If we start shooting, there's no telling who else might show up to the party. How far is your pa's place anyway?'

'Half a day or a day maybe. I don't know for sure. It's been a while.'

For the first time, doubt crept into Daniel's mind. 'How long is it since you were there?'

'Ten years, give or take.'

He had been about to make a move towards the horses, but he held back. 'Come again?'

Now he saw stubbornness in the set

of her mouth. 'When Pa brought me out this way, he told me to remember it.'

'Well, this just gets better.'

'I'm good at remembering things. I can find the place. I just don't know how long it'll take.'

Daniel turned his attention back to the riders. They didn't seem to be in any hurry, which could mean they didn't believe she was a threat or that they were familiar with the trail and confident they could chase her down before she reached safety.

He wiped sweat from his forehead, noticing that his injured arm felt heavy and weak. When he flexed his fingers, they too seemed less flexible. Whether use would improve or worsen the situation, he had no idea.

'Do you see that?' Charlie asked. 'I think there's another rider out there.'

Daniel followed the direction of her pointing finger. Although some distance behind the first two, this man was gaining.

'Two against three. How do you like those odds?' he asked.

'I think we should ride.'

Being careful not to skyline themselves, they contoured the rim before dropping back down into a narrow canyon. Once they had crossed that, the miles and hours slipped by slowly with them following a series of switch-backs that took them deeper into the mountains.

Daniel had expected Charlie would show some hesitation when faced with the maze of canyons and gullies that branched off the main trail, but she led with conviction, ever alert. If she had any doubts, they didn't show. Only when the ground became rockier, the trail narrower and less defined due to numerous heavy rock falls, did she drop back to ride alongside him.

'We're close. Be ready for anything.'

Daniel flexed the fingers on his right hand. They were no stiffer but his arm had been throbbing for the past hour and it ached to the shoulder whenever he moved it. Holding a rifle was difficult, lifting it was downright precarious and he shoved the Henry back into its boot.

'Good idea,' she said, following suit with the Yellow Boy. 'We'll be in their sights before we could get off a shot anyway.'

A chill ran along Daniel's spine despite the sheen of sweat that made the woollen shirt cling to his skin. Whatever happened, they were trapped now. Unknown assailants behind. An uncertain welcome ahead.

He tried to relax, but the ache in his head and the throbbing in his arm acted like harbingers of doom. With the landscape rising higher around them, the path narrowing in places so that the horses had to inch through, misgivings began to surface.

'Are you sure this is the way? It doesn't look like anyone's been here for a while, forever maybe.'

'It wouldn't be much of a hideout if anyone could find it, would it?' She smiled. 'You've trusted me this far, don't lose faith now.'

But within minutes, they hit a dead end.

16

They had been riding single file through an area of heavy rock fall. Now, the trail opened out to about fifty feet but they were faced with walls on three sides, rising endlessly towards an empty sky. Charlie rode in a wide circle, first one way and then the other, while Daniel mentally traced the route that had brought them there, finding no obvious place where they could have veered off the trail, if that's what it had been.

At last, Charlie stopped circling, bringing Red round to stand beside his grey. Like Daniel, she craned her neck to survey the high walls that trapped them.

'We should go back,' Daniel said, 'try to find where we lost the trail. If those riders were following us, they can't be far behind by now and we don't want to be trapped.'

She placed her hand on his before he could flick the reins. 'Just wait.'

He looked over his shoulder. Had he heard something or was it his imagination? Either way, they couldn't stay there much longer. His gaze had scanned the area more than once and he saw no way in or out except that by which they had entered.

'Look,' she whispered.

Daniel saw the shotgun before he saw the man behind it. Like a chameleon changing its colours, he separated himself from the rock face to stand directly ahead of them at least twenty feet above ground level. With things falling into perspective, Daniel guessed there was a ledge, probably deep enough that, along with the height advantage, the lookout could hide his position merely by stepping away from the edge.

Hatless and wearing a faded black shirt and pants, the shaggy-haired old outlaw regarded them along the barrel of the rifle. 'State your business.'

'We're here to see the boss.' Charlie knocked back her hat. 'I'm Charlie Wells of the Crooked-W and this is my friend Daniel Cliff. We're in trouble and we need sanctuary.'

'How'd you find this place?'

'I've been here before. Ten years ago, maybe.'

'Ten years?' The lookout raised an eyebrow. 'My memory never was much good but let me see if I can remember . . . ' He stroked his chin thoughtfully. 'All right then, if I said, one, two, buckle my shoe, you'd say?'

'Three, four, knock-knock-knock on the door.'

He lowered his rifle and nodded thoughtfully. 'Well, I'll be damned. I don't know how you managed to find this place, or how you came across that particular old phrase, but here you are. I guess you better come on in and we'll see what the boss has to say. Do you know the way?'

'I think so.'

Charlie started Red forward towards

the rocks but when Daniel started to follow the lookout raised his rifle. 'Not you.'

'He's with me.'

'I don't know him and he seems a mite nervous. Is there someone else out there I should know about?'

'Two, maybe three men,' Daniel admitted.

'Friends of yours?'

'No. They've been trailing us since daybreak. Could be they were just naturally heading this way but, after the trouble we've had, it seems unlikely.'

The lookout cussed. 'Girl, you go on. Wait for me on the other side. Don't go no further, if you know what's good for you. We don't get women up here.'

'What about him?'

'He'll be along when we've taken care of business.'

'But — '

'No buts. You brought trouble with you. I can't let just anybody ride into this place and I ain't taking on three guns alone. Just be grateful I don't kill you for being stupid. Now, go! A gunfight ain't no place for a woman.'

Daniel didn't like it. He rested his hand on the Smith & Wesson, but didn't remove it from the holster. His fingers felt stiff and tight, like he was wearing a glove that was too small. He looked over his shoulder. This time he heard movement for sure. His horse moved uneasily, sensing another animal or maybe feeling his fear.

He wondered what it would take to get past the lookout. If his arm was in better shape, shooting his way in might be an option, but not a good one. Especially when he didn't even know where the entrance was.

'You go. I'll be right behind you,' he told Charlie, sounding more confident than he felt.

With a nod, she urged Red forward. When she looked about to hit the rock face, she turned him sharply to the left and horse and rider disappeared as if into thin air.

17

'That's some illusion, ain't it?' the lookout said. 'If you don't know it's there, you'd never see it.' He raised his rifle and aimed it at Daniel. 'Now why don't you tell me who you really are, mister?'

'My name's Daniel Cliff.'

The man shook his head. 'The woman might believe that, but Dan Cliff's a good friend of mine and you ain't him by about twenty years, I'd say.'

Daniel sighed. 'If you know him . . . ' He pushed back his hat so that the lookout could see the resemblance. 'You'll see I'm telling the truth.'

The man's eyes widened. 'Well, I'll be damned, if you ain't a dead ringer.'

'We'll both be damned if those riders find this place.'

The lookout inclined his ear towards

the trail. This time there was no mistaking the sound of company.

'Coming in,' someone shouted. 'Don't shoot.'

'You keep your hands where I can see them and I won't need to.'

A single rider emerged into the open, his hands resting on the pommel of his saddle. He glanced in Daniel's direction before returning his attention to the man on the ledge.

'We're friends,' he said, inclining his head towards the man who stayed behind him. 'Go ahead and ask me.'

The lookout considered. 'Fair enough, why not? If I said, one two, buckle my shoe, you'd say?'

The newcomer's mouth twitched into a smile. 'Three, four knock on the door.'

A shot exploded as the lookout fired without warning. His bullet hit the man high in the chest and he fell from the saddle, dangling with his boot heel caught in the stirrup. Panicked, his horse backed out of the confined space, dragging its dead rider along with it. Another quick shot, and a scream confirmed another hit.

Daniel hadn't touched his gun. There hadn't been time. The lookout's defence had been so quick, cold and deliberate. As he looked with disbelief at the man, he cocked his ear, listening to the sound of retreating horses.

'Son-of-a-bitch, I only winged that second bastard,' the lookout said. 'Ben's going to be in an ugly mood when he catches up with him.'

He fired three evenly spaced shots into the air.

'He won't get far now,' he said, meeting Daniel's stare. 'What? You didn't think this place only had one guard, did you?'

Just then, shots rang out, not too distant. Daniel watched the lookout count to five on his fingers as he cocked an ear to the sky. On six, three evenly spaced shots followed.

'Goddamn, he's good. I hope he caught those horses.'

They waited. Daniel's arm throbbed like a clock marking time, seeming to rock his whole body. He pulled irritably at the front of his shirt. It was damp and clingy.

'What are we waiting for?' he asked.

The lookout pressed a finger to his lips, his eyes never leaving the entrance.

Daniel wondered what had happened to Charlie. Had she heard the shots and assumed he was dead? Would she care? Or had something happened to her? Even now was she fighting for her life against some deranged outlaw?

The sound of hoofs approaching dragged him back to his own situation.

'Comin' in,' someone shouted.

The lookout started to bring his rifle up but lowered it when the rider appeared leading two saddled horses each with a body thrown across the saddle.

'Well, I'll be damned,' he said. 'I didn't expect to see you back in these parts.'

'Ah didn't expect to be back, Frank.'

The newcomer turned to Daniel and grinned, showing a gap between his front teeth that seemed in keeping with his twisted nose and black eyes. 'Ah'm guessin' you'll be Daniel Cliff.'

Daniel wracked his memory, certain he'd remember a face like that, but with his head pounding in time with the pain in his arm, he couldn't place it.

'Do I know you?'

'No, sir, you don't,' he replied in a thick Texan drawl, 'but Ma told me you were with Charlie and not to shoot you, which makes me happy to see you alive because ah wasn't taking names when that *hombre* opened fire on me.' He walked the horses past. 'Now are you comin' in or did you come all this way just to sit there?'

Daniel glanced towards the lookout but the man had already stepped back from the edge and disappeared. Prodding his horse, he followed the newcomer, almost colliding with the cliff face before he glimpsed an opening to his left, wide enough for one horse and rider but situated at such an acute angle that until you were right on top of it, it was impossible to see. Turning his horse sharply, he found himself in a narrow tunnel, high walled and open to the sky but no more than five or six feet wide and one hundred feet long, that opened out into a lush meadow.

By the time he saw the men holding Charlie, their guns were already cocked and aimed at him and it was too late to do anything.

18

Charlie couldn't believe her eyes.

'Al?'

He grinned. 'In the flesh.'

'I thought . . . '

He smiled his crooked smile at her. 'Ah guess we've both got questions, but now ain't the time for askin' 'em. Best we get you to the boss first.'

Beyond the meadow and through a sparse stand of trees, the outlaw camp sprang up like a small town. Although the buildings were weathered now, she recognized the old bathhouse, the store-cum-saloon, and the livery stable. But, since she had been gone, a new bunkhouse and a canteen had been added. About twenty horses grazed in a corral built on the surrounding grassland.

Higher up, against the backdrop of the mountain and situated away from the rest of the buildings, she saw the log cabin where she had spent the first few years of her life. Its slotted construction and mud-finished roof appeared to have stood the test of time well. However, the smokeless chimney, shuttered windows and broken-down fence gave it a stark, uninhabited feel. Not the way she remembered it.

As the small group neared the centre of the trail, two men came out of the saloon, glasses in their hands. Both in their late forties, smartly dressed in wool pants, coloured flannel shirts, leather vests, and carrying Stetsons, they each ran a careful eye over the newcomers.

'What have we got here, boys?'

The question sounded friendly enough.

Charlie's eyes fixed on the man in front. He was tall, over six feet, and broad in the chest. His thin blond hair was shot through heavily with grey and deep lines etched the skin around his eyes and the corners of his thin mouth.

Cold blue eyes studied her curiously.

'Pa?'

He stepped forward into the late afternoon sunshine, squinting up at her. His mouth moved silently and then he said, 'Charlotte?'

'Yes, Pa, it's me.' She pushed her hat back to hang by its string. 'Charlie.'

No one tried to stop her when she dismounted but when she moved towards him, he stepped back and raised his hand, stalling her in her tracks.

Charlie sensed a dozen or more men appearing on the street around them. She felt like a juicy steak placed before a hungry man as old and young alike openly leered. Others eyed the newcomers with a mixture of interest and animosity.

Her pa looked past her. 'Al, what's she doing here?'

Charlie looked between them, her confusion matched by the surprise on Al's face. It seemed both of them had secrets and now that she thought about it, she kicked herself for not realizing sooner. When Al had appeared from the tunnel, he had merely nodded an acknowledgement to the men holding her. She hadn't given it much thought at the time, stunned as she was to see him alive, but now it made sense.

He was one of them.

'How do you know each other?' she asked.

'Al's the best horse thief I ever hired.' Her pa nodded at the bodies thrown over the horses. 'It looks like you had some trouble.'

'You could say that, Mr Wells,' Al agreed. 'These *hombres* were following Charlie.'

'What about him?' Wells asked, transferring his full attention to Daniel. 'He doesn't look too good. Is he with you or one of them?'

'He came up with Charlie.'

She helped Daniel climb down from his horse, supporting his weight across her shoulders while he caught his balance. Heat radiated from him like a fire and his clothes, she noticed, felt damp.

'He took a beating helping me get away from Scott Johnson. It's a long story,' she said. 'He needs his wounds tending and some rest, that's all.'

The second man stepped forward, tossing his drink aside. He bore a close resemblance to Daniel, except for the lines on his face, an extra twenty pounds and a scar along his left cheekbone.

'Roy, I think we better continue this reunion up at the house, don't you?'

Charlie chose to keep her eyes fixed on her pa but she had sensed more than seen the crowd moving in like a pack of wolves.

Roy Wells glanced around then waved at the two gunmen who had accompanied the newcomers from the tunnel. 'You boys take the horses to the corral, tell Cookie to bring some food up to the house, then you bury those bodies. The rest of you,' he shouted, 'get back about your business. Nothing here concerns you.'

* * *

It took a minute for her eyes to adjust to the low light in the cabin but as Charlie looked around, it was as she remembered. A large open area with a table and chairs at one end, a wood-burning stove in the corner, and a fire-place on the back wall flanked on either side by a couple of stuffed, hide-covered chairs each with a side table on which stood empty glasses and a half bottle of whiskey. Two doors closed off the main area from the bedrooms.

Al opened the shutters then lit the stove and started a pot of coffee. Charlie helped Daniel to a chair at the table, removing his hat as his chin sagged to his chest. Her pa and the other man hung back outside, their heads close together as they gesticulated between the cabin and the other buildings.

'Hang in there,' Charlie said, touching Daniel's cheek. It felt hot and his smile barely registered. She turned back to the others. 'Do you have any — '

A hand grabbed her arm, pulling her off balance as she was swung forcefully around.

'Let me take a good look at you, girl.' Her pa's smile lit up his face as his eyes took her in, his fingers stroking her hair. 'It's good to see you after all this time. You've grown into a fine-looking woman.'

'You're not mad?'

'Mad? No, not mad.' He beckoned to the other man who was pouring whiskey into a glass. 'Dan, get over here, say hello to my little girl.'

Diligently, Dan ambled over and removed his hat. Again, Charlie was taken aback by his similarity to Daniel, only now she could really see him, she could see the differences too.

'This is Dan Cliff, my right-hand man.'

His lips twitched, resembling a smile. 'Pleased to meet you.'

Charlie doubted it. His hard gaze met

hers for no more than a moment but it was enough for her to see something unfriendly in their dark depths.

Charlie placed her hand on Daniel's shoulder. 'And this is my friend, Daniel Cliff.'

Daniel raised his head, getting slowly to his feet, using the table for support. 'Hello, Dad,' he said, with unconcealed bitterness. 'Remember me, you son of a bitch?'

Before the older man could say a word, Daniel's fist caught him across the jaw. It jarred the outlaw but almost as if he had been expecting it, he countered with a left to Daniel's stomach that doubled him over and lined him up for a vicious punch to the chin that snapped his head back and knocked him down.

'He's out cold,' Charlie said, dropping to her knees and patting Daniel's cheek.

'He threw the first punch. What was I supposed to do?' Dan asked, reasonably.

'You might have killed him.'

Dan nodded. 'Well, make sure he knows that when he wakes up.'

19

Daniel woke with a thirst like nothing he'd ever felt before. His eyelids flickered, fighting to focus in the dim light. The room was stuffy, with no sign of a window. The only light coming in was through a crack in the open door. Beyond he could hear raised voices.

'You should have told me he was your pa.'

'Like you should have told me you were a horse thief?'

'Would you have given me a job if ah had?'

'No.'

'That's why ah didn't tell you.'

'Well, maybe you should have. It would have saved us both a lot of heartache. You better go before my pa gets back.'

'Nothin's changed, Charlie, not for me. Ah care about you, ah really do.'

'Everything's changed, Al.'

Daniel tried to push up onto his elbow, moaning when pain shot along his arm and across his ribs. It was difficult to tell which hurt more and he flopped back down, resting his throbbing head lightly against the hard pillow before forcing his breathing into a shallow, controlled rhythm.

He came awake with a jolt, struggling to breathe. It was almost dark. Blinking rapidly, he cleared the nightmare that had seen him facing off against green eyes filled with murderous intent.

'I know Val Johnson,' a man was saying beyond the open door. It was a different voice to before. 'He rode with me and Roy for a while in the early days, but he was a stone-cold killer and Roy didn't want that kind of reputation dogging him.'

'Tom never said anything to me about that.'

Daniel recognized Charlie's voice.

'Why would he? Tom and Roy were like strangers. It was the way they both wanted it. That's why Tom changed his name to Mason after Roy left. It's unlikely he even knew about Johnson's connection to your pa.'

'Maybe if Johnson had known . . . '

'Things would have been different? And maybe not. We've always given each other plenty of room, but it's been a long time and sometimes an itch just has to be scratched.'

'An itch?' Charlie asked. 'You mean an old score?'

'He's an odd bird. It's hard to say what motivates him.'

Daniel heard a door bang but when he opened his eyes again, a bright shaft of light greeted him. In the next room, he could see Charlie sitting at a table. Was she sewing? He thought he must be dreaming, but when he tried to call out, she came to him.

'You're awake at last,' she said, dropping to her knees beside him before handing him a glass of water. 'Drink this before you try to speak.'

She waited for him to take a sip.

'Sorry about the accommodation,' she said, motioning to the shelves stacked with tins and other provisions, and sacks of grain and flour piled up on the floor. 'This used to be my room but Pa turned it into a storeroom after . . . well, anyway, he let me put a mattress on the floor for you. How are you feeling? You've been asleep for more than thirty-six hours.'

'I'm not sure. What happened?'

'You mean after you took a swing at Dan, I mean, your pa?'

'Did I?'

'You tried. Luckily for you, you were running a fever from that dirty spur you took to your arm and all you really did was fall on him.'

Daniel drank some more water. 'How did he take it?'

'I'm not sure. He doesn't say much, but my pa thought it was hilarious.' She looked thoughtful. 'When I'm talking to you, should I call your pa Dan, or should I call him your pa?'

'He hasn't been a pa to me for

twenty-two years.'

He could see his bitterness threw up more questions but she didn't press him and he was grateful for that. His head was already starting to ache again.

'Pa'll be back in a few minutes,' she said, getting to her feet. 'He's been waiting for you to come round. He wants to talk to you.'

'Then I better not keep him waiting.' He noticed his pants, shirt and boots at the foot of the bed. 'Did I just see you with a needle and thread in your hand?'

'Uh-huh. Pa told me to make some curtains to cover the windows.'

'I thought you couldn't sew.'

'I can't to speak of.'

He touched his injured arm tentatively. It was lightly bandaged and sore, but at least it wasn't throbbing anymore. 'You didn't sew me up, did you?'

'No.'

He sighed with feigned relief. 'Good. I don't want my arm falling off,' he said, with a wink.

* * *

Roy Wells had a reputation as a badman. His operation had been successful for more than fifteen years. A careful planner and recruiter, he had masterminded more than twenty bank and railroad robberies in that time. Few had resulted in casualties and those that did rarely attached themselves to his name. His identity remained largely undocumented, although various ambiguous descriptions existed on numerous wanted posters across the country. Only a handful of men knew the location of the Wells Gang and, as Daniel had already found out, security was tight.

He thought about all this while he watched the man of legend laughing with his daughter. In her presence, the harsh lines on his face softened, the loud boom of his voice quieted just a little.

And yet still Daniel sensed danger.

'So, what are your plans now, Daniel?' he asked, after pushing his empty breakfast plate away.

'I hadn't really thought about it.'

Roy took a few minutes to roll a cigarette, light it and savour the flavour of the tobacco as he eyed Daniel across the table.

'Were you hoping for a spot on my crew?'

'I was just trying to help your daughter.'

'That's not the whole truth, is it?' His eyes turned hard. 'I'm guessing you came here to see your pa.'

There seemed no point in denying it. 'I did want to meet him.'

'With what intention?'

'With respect, sir, that's between me and him.'

Roy looked amused. 'Maybe, but Dan's my partner. If your intentions are, shall we say, detrimental to my plans, I might have something to say about that.'

'I didn't come here to kill him, if that's what you mean.'

Wells laughed. 'Good, because as I

understand it, you've become a good friend to my girl here.'

Pouring coffee into her pa's cup, Charlie nodded. 'He saved my life. Friends don't come any better than that.'

Roy patted her hand, condescendingly Daniel thought.

'I'll bear that in mind.'

He shoved to his feet, the light from the window throwing him into silhouette and obscuring his features. It didn't make him any less imposing. He was a big man in any light.

'Walk with me to the door, Dan Junior.'

'Just Daniel.'

'Have it your way.'

When they were out of earshot of Charlie, Roy lowered his head, speaking close and quiet. 'Bar this door when I leave and stay away from the windows. Don't let anybody in or out unless you know them.'

'Am I a prisoner?'

Roy's smile was disingenuous. 'Until

I say otherwise, you're a guest, but there are things you should understand. I run a tight crew and they don't like outsiders. It creates tension.'

He reached behind a coat hanging from a nail on the wall, and handed Daniel's gun and belt to him.

'I'm giving this back to you for protection. Not yours. I don't give a damn about you, but she likes you so for now we'll play things out and see where they lead. That gun's for her protection. The men respect me, but at the end of the day, they're outlaws. Men on the wrong side of the law with nothing to lose. Desperate characters separated from basic pleasures. Do you understand me?'

Daniel nodded.

'Then understand this, you raise that gun against anybody that ain't aiming to do her harm, and I'll kill you. You lay a hand on her, and I'll kill you.'

Daniel felt his hackles rise but, for now, he simply nodded.

Roy put on his hat and opened the

door. The sun felt warm on Daniel's face, the air fresh and clean after the stuffiness of the storeroom. The blue sky seemed to mock him with its distance.

'The men'll be leavin' in the next week. Until then, she doesn't go outside and nobody comes in.'

'And after that?' Daniel asked, an unpleasant suspicion picking at the edges of his mind.

'Now that's the million dollar question, ain't it?'

20

Over the next few days, Roy's visits were infrequent. Although initially he had seemed to enjoy the company of his daughter, it appeared to Daniel that he was becoming bored with her. When she talked, he didn't seem to listen. The harsh lines around his mouth and eyes didn't soften now when he laughed and his tone was abrupt. He barely finished a cup of coffee before he had to leave.

His exchanges with Daniel were mostly hushed, not for Charlie's ears, and amounted to threats of what would happen if any harm came to her. Daniel couldn't really blame him. She was a pretty girl with a sweet disposition, woman enough to turn any man's head.

Still, Roy's continuing hostility irked him. As did the failure of his own pa to put in an appearance. It gnawed at him like a dog with a bone, building on years of resentment already deep-rooted in his being. He found himself frequently looking out of the window, hoping for a glimpse of the man who had abandoned his mother.

Today more than usual, he resented the situation. Maybe it was the cloying heat inside the cabin, the breeze through the open windows barely stirring the air. Feeling restless, he went to stand in the doorway where he could look out along what constituted the main street of the outlaw camp. Even with the evening sun shining on the clutter of ramshackle buildings it didn't make them seem any less hostile.

He studied the layout. Opposite the canteen was the saloon, beside that the bathhouse and further along, the livery stable and corral where he could just make out his and Charlie's horses amongst a dozen others. Behind the canteen were two bunkhouses, one of which looked to have fallen into disrepair with the roof caved in at one end.

'What are you looking at?' Charlie asked, peering over his shoulder.

'Just looking.'

She eased into the doorway and raised her hand to shield her eyes against the setting sun. After days of being shut inside the cabin, she looked noticeably pale and tired. It was no surprise. He had heard her tossing and turning in the night, unable to sleep without any activity to tire her during the day. Now that he was on the mend, he felt it too.

At least if they were in prison, they would have work to do.

She touched his arm. 'I'm sorry.'

'For what?'

'For getting you into this. I know you don't want to be here. You're like a caged mountain lion.'

He smiled. 'It's nothing against your company.'

'But I know how you feel. Being kept in a cabin like a prisoner, it isn't what I expected.' She shrugged. 'Maybe some things are better left as a memory.'

They stood for a long while, just watching the sky grow darker, feeling the night chill to a bearable temperature. Below, torches were lit and men moved from building to building. With nothing else to do, they headed back inside.

* * *

'Do you hear that?' Charlie asked later as she shuffled her last losing hand into a worn deck of cards. 'It sounds like a harpsichord . . . and a violin . . . and . . . singing?'

'It does,' Daniel agreed. 'It sounds like quite a shindig going on down there.'

She got up from the table and went to the window. The curtain had been pulled across and she opened it to look out into the night. Down the hill, fires had been lit between the buildings and she could see movement, men crossing between the saloon and the canteen.

'I guess they're letting off steam before they leave.' She closed the curtain. 'Do you dance?'

'Do I what?'

'Dance.' She tapped her toes to demonstrate as she walked towards him. 'You know, jig.'

'No.'

He shook his head but she caught his hand, swinging it gently as she coaxed him out of his chair and started into a rhythmic sway.

'You know I'm recovering from a really severe beating, don't you?' he said with mock seriousness.

'It's been more than a week. You can't play that card forever. Besides, this'll help your recovery and I'll go easy on you, I promise.'

True to her word, she did most of the work, but as she danced around him, moving to the quick rhythm of the distant music, his toes started to tap. In no time at all, he was spinning her around and laughing as much as she was. It felt good. She felt invigorated. The weight of the past week's confinement seemed to lift with each step. For the first time in days, she forgot about Val Johnson, the Crooked-W, Billy and Uncle Tom and where she was.

There was only music and dancing and laughter.

And then angry banging.

'What the Hell's going on in there? Open this door.'

Before Daniel had the bar lifted off completely, the door swung open and her pa filled the frame. He burst in and looked around the room. What he was expecting to see, Charlie couldn't imagine. That he suspected something inappropriate was apparent as he narrowed his eyes at them.

'We heard the music,' Charlie said, breathlessly. 'We were just — '

'You get out,' he said, pointing at Daniel. 'I need to speak to my daughter and it doesn't concern you.'

He shoved him outside and slammed the door. Crossing the room in a couple of long strides, he grabbed Charlie roughly by the arm.

'We can talk about what's been going

on here later,' he said, his gaze sweeping the room again. 'But first, what's this I hear about you and Al Dawson?'

An unpleasant chill washed over Charlie as her father towered menacingly over her. In that instant, she understood why men feared him. With nostrils flared and lips curled back over his teeth, he looked like a wolf ready to attack. His fingers bit into her flesh with vicelike intensity.

'You're hurting me,' she said, trying to wriggle free.

He didn't relent. 'Al's down there telling anybody who'll listen that you're his girl, that you and him are going to be married.' He shook her. 'Well?'

'We talked about it, but . . . '

'But what?'

'We hadn't spoken to Uncle Tom, got his blessing.'

'His blessing?' He thumbed his chest. 'What about my blessing?'

She started to tremble. 'I thought you were dead.'

'Well now you know different, and

I'm telling you what I told him. No daughter of mine is marrying a horse thief. Do you understand me?'

She nodded.

'You keep away from him.'

His voice had lowered, losing some of its thunder, and he released her arm. She noticed him flex the fingers of his right hand. The knuckles were cut and smeared with blood.

'Did you do something to him?'

'That's none of your concern. You just do what I say and keep away from him.'

A sudden burst of anger and frustration surged to the surface. Since her arrival he had shown no interest in her life outside the hideout. The death of Billy and her uncle didn't seem to bother him. The loss of the ranch barely raised an eyebrow. Yet the loose tongue of a gentle man had, by outward appearances, sent him into a violent rage.

'Why did you send him to the Crooked-W?' she asked before she could stop herself.

She braced for the backlash, automatically turning her face away from him as she waited for the weight of his big hand to fall on her.

Instead, he said, 'I couldn't have him on my crew any longer. He was becoming a liability. He needed a place to lie low and I heard the Crooked-W needed a bronc-buster after Tom had his accident. It seemed like a reasonable plan.' He took a deep breath as his anger flared. 'I sure as Hell didn't expect you to take a shine to him, but from what I've just seen maybe you've got an eye for men, like your mother had.'

She didn't like the insinuation. 'I was brought up by a man, among men. They've always treated me with respect, and Al and Daniel are no different. Yes, I care for Al, but after what's happened, things will never be the same again and marriage to any man seems like a distant dream now. I hope that makes you happy.'

He smiled and, like a chameleon, the monster that had raged within him was gone. He lifted her hand, holding it tenderly between both of his. 'You're a good girl. I'm sorry if I frightened you, but you heed my words and put all romantic thoughts about Al away.'

She gave a single nod, unwilling to give in completely.

'Good, now have you got a cup of coffee for your old pa?'

Charlie fetched it, handing it to him without her usual cordial smile. For a few seconds, he stared into her face, a thoughtful look on his.

'You look like your mother when you're afraid. She wasn't strong enough for this place, but you just might be.' He shook his head. 'What am I going to do with you, Charlotte?'

Holed up in the cabin for the past week, the question had crossed her mind too. She was wise enough to know why he was keeping her away from his men, but if he didn't trust them around her, what future was there for her here in this remote hideout?

'I'd like to go home,' she said.

'How do you plan on doing that? The Crooked-W's gone.'

'It can be rebuilt.'

'And what about Val Johnson? He's not a man given to changing his mind.'

'I think he deserves to pay for what he's done. You've got enough men to see to that.'

He laughed. 'It's not worth it.'

'Not worth it? He murdered Billy and Uncle Tom and half a dozen men who did nothing to deserve it. Don't they deserve some justice?'

'It's an admirable sentiment but my life is here.'

'Well, mine isn't. I can't live like a prisoner. The only life I know is back there, and that's your doing. If you won't — '

He held up his hand for silence, not to stop whatever threat she had been about to make, but to listen to the sound of voices and scuffling coming from outside. Moving swiftly to the door, he swung it open and stepped out.

Charlie followed, emerging behind him just as Daniel landed a punch that sent Dan Cliff smashing headlong into Roy.

'What the Hell's going on, Dan?' Roy shouted. 'I told you to stay the Hell away from him.'

'You did, but this is one time I've got to make up my own mind,' Dan said, seemingly unworried by his partner's tone. 'So, if you'll just step back, me and my son have got a few things we need to get straight.'

Charlie tried to squeeze past but as her pa thrust Dan back into the fight, his other arm circled her neck and held her back.

'Let it play out,' he said. 'It's high time we decide what to do with young Daniel anyway.'

Daniel's breathing sounded ragged, and he was shielding his ribs with his hand.

'It isn't a fair fight, he's hurt,' she said.

'This is what he came here for. Let him go at it.'

As father and son circled, looking for an opportunity, Charlie noticed that her pa loosened his Colt in its holster.

'What are you doing?'

'Be quiet, girl. This doesn't concern you.'

Charlie watched as Dan feinted a left to the stomach, striking Daniel on the chin with a right-left combination.

Like a cat playing with a mouse, he waited until his son regained his senses.

Daniel blocked another right but missed the left that smashed him in the stomach, doubling him over and almost bringing him to his knees.

Again, Dan waited for him to stand up.

Daniel spat on the ground. 'Ma said you were a hard man.'

Dan grinned. 'She was a good judge of character.'

Dan went for another punch to the jaw but this time Daniel countered and landed a shot of his own. It glanced off

Dan's temple, hard enough to cause the older man to stop and cuss.

'But she loved you until the day she died,' Daniel continued. 'I never understood it. That's why I wanted to find you. I wanted you to be sorry for the way you treated her.'

'I ain't ever been sorry about the way I treated any woman.'

'She wasn't just any woman. She was your wife.'

Dan shrugged.

'She bore you a son.'

'That was her burden to carry, not mine. She wanted it that way.'

Something seemed to snap in Daniel then. With an almighty roar he lunged headfirst, hitting Dan in the legs and bringing him down. The older man wrestled him off, both of them coming to their feet, fists swinging, each giving and taking violent blows that sprayed blood and crunched bone.

At last, both winded, they came apart.

'Did your ma teach you to fight?'

Dan asked, breathing hard and spitting blood. 'You hit like a girl.' He pointed at the Smith & Wesson in its holster. 'Are you any better with that?'

Charlie winced as her pa's fingers bit into her shoulder. She glimpsed his hand close on the Colt, and looked up to see a smile she didn't like or trust.

'Daniel, don't,' she shouted. 'They're going to kill you.'

But father and son were already poised for action. She had seen it once before when two of Johnson's gunslingers faced off outside the Lucky Diamond. She doubted they were even aware of their surroundings, focused as they were on each other.

But she had to try to stop them.

As hard as she could, she stamped on her pa's foot, at the same time biting into his hand. His grip loosened. Instantly, she dropped and scrambled away to throw herself in front of Daniel.

She saw Dan's gaze flicker, a queer look pass over his face, as if he was waking from a trance.

'That's enough.' Roy stepped between them. 'You two said your piece. It's done. Do I make myself clear?'

Both men nodded.

Roy glared at his daughter, his mouth pulled into a tight line of disapproval. 'You had me fooled for a while there, Charlotte. I thought maybe you were like me, but now I see I was wrong. You're your mother's daughter through and through. Soft and weak.'

'I'm happy to disappoint you.'

He spat on the ground. 'Clean him up and get him a blanket, if you want to. He sleeps outside from now on.'

21

The following morning, sitting with her back against the wall of the cabin, soaking in the sun's therapeutic rays, Charlie cast a sideways glance at Daniel. His face was a patchwork of bruises and cuts, although thankfully there were no broken bones.

'Your pa's coming, you should go inside,' he said, nodding towards a figure tramping up the hill.

She didn't move, instead steeling herself for whatever Roy Wells had in store for them today. But he looked surprisingly friendly as he walked unhurriedly to join them.

'I think we should clear the air before I leave,' he said, sounding unexpectedly pleasant. 'It seems to me I underestimated you, Daniel. That business between you and your pa, it wasn't any of my concern.'

He paused, as if waiting for some agreement, but Daniel remained non-committal.

'As it stands between us, I gave you a job to do and you've done it. No more, no less. I need men around me who can take orders. When I get back, we should talk about you becoming a member of my crew.'

Again he waited for some response but Daniel stayed quiet.

'You will be here when I get back, won't you?'

'Do I have a choice?'

Charlie held her breath.

Roy's laughter sounded forced. 'Nobody's keeping you here.'

He turned to his daughter and, dropping to his haunches, took her hands between his, gently stroking her fingers. 'And you, Charlotte, while I'm gone I want you to decide what you want to do. I'm a wealthy man, you could travel if you wanted, or I could set you up on a little ranch somewhere if that's more to your liking.'

He was quite charming when he wanted to be, but memories of the way he might have murdered Daniel were too raw. She fought the urge to pull away and smiled as brightly as she could muster.

'I'd like that.'

'I knew you would. Now give your pa a hug before he leaves.'

Again, she resisted the urge to balk and wrapped her arms around him, counting to ten before easing away.

'Once me and the boys ride out,' Roy said, settling his hat, 'you're both free to roam around the camp. Daniel, you move into the bunkhouse. I'll be leaving a few men behind but I trust them and Charlotte will be safe.'

Daniel nodded.

'I'll be back in about three days.' He reached out and offered Daniel his hand. 'Here's to new beginnings, eh?'

After they shook on it, he walked away, whistling.

'Did you believe any of that?' Charlie asked, a shiver running through her.

'Not really.'

'Then we need to leave. Today. The sooner we go, the further we can get away from here before they realize we're gone.'

They put together some supplies from the storeroom and waited an hour after the men rode out. It was easy to see them leave from the vantage point of the cabin on the hill. Then side-by-side, they walked down to the clutter of buildings, checking each one in turn for company. Finding no one about, they made their way to the stable.

Both horses were in the corral, but there didn't seem to be anyone around.

'The saddles must be inside somewhere,' Charlie said. 'I'll take a look.'

Walking inside, she allowed her eyes time to adjust to the reduced light. The twenty or so stalls stood empty, and as with the other buildings this one seemed deserted. Walking past the stalls, she peered into each one as she searched for the saddles. At last, she spied hers hanging near the back and hurried forward, her heart sinking a little when she saw the empty rifle boot.

'Charlie?'

She had been about to lift the saddle but now she froze.

'Who said that?'

'In here.'

Cautiously, she peered into the last stall.

* * *

Daniel was glad to see the grey looking rested and well fed. Someone had been taking good care of both horses. Their coats gleamed and their manes and tails had been brushed free of tangles. On seeing him, both looked eager to be set free of their confinement and vied for his attention.

After a few minutes, he looked towards the stable, wondering what was keeping Charlie. He wandered across to the entrance and peered inside. There was no sign of her.

'Charlie?'

'I'm here.'

He drew his gun, alarmed by the strained tone of her voice. 'Are you all right?'

'Yes. I'm with Al. He's hurt.'

Daniel followed her voice, checking each stall he passed. He wasn't prepared to take any chances. For all he knew, Al could be holding a gun to Charlie's head, but when he rounded the last stall, Charlie was kneeling in the straw beside him.

He looked to have had a thorough beating. One eye was swollen almost shut, his lips were covered in dried blood and his arm lay at an unnatural angle. His shirt was torn and Daniel could see more bruises over his body.

'That bad?' Al asked, seeing his expression.

'Not pretty.'

'Ah've had worse from a stubborn bronc. Help me up, would you?'

Daniel holstered his gun and slipped his arm under Al's uninjured arm.

Together they manoeuvred him onto his feet and leaned him against the wall where he stood breathing hard.

‘Charlie, honey,’ he said through short breaths. ‘Ah’m sorry, you’re going to have to saddle your own horse today.’

‘Oh Al, don’t worry about that. I’m not even thinking about it.’

‘Ah’m not worried.’ He smiled. ‘But you should be. You can’t stay here, obviously you know that or you wouldn’t be creepin’ around.’ He winced. ‘Your rifles are out back, hidden under some old blankets. Why don’t you fetch them while ah catch my breath?’

She seemed reluctant to leave him. For the first time since he had known her, Daniel saw tears in her eyes.

‘He’ll be all right,’ he said. ‘Just give him a minute or two.’

When she was gone, Al pulled himself up straight.

‘Thanks. Ah didn’t want her to see me like this. Did you ever pop a shoulder back in?’

'Nope.' And Daniel didn't relish the thought of doing it now.

'Give me some room then.'

Leaning forward on his left leg, Al let his arm dangle then slowly and carefully shifted his weight up, leaning back and rotating his shoulders. Fresh blood bubbled on his lips as he bit down against the pain. Minutes passed and then there was a slight pop.

Daniel caught him as he staggered. 'Was that it?'

'Uh huh. Works every time but hurts like Hell. Ah didn't want her to see it.' He nodded towards two saddles. 'Do you mind saddlin' up for me?'

'You're coming with us then?'

'Have you got a problem with that?'

In all honesty, he did. Al could barely stand.

Al chuckled. 'Don't worry about me. Ah'm a bronc-buster, this is just me on a bad day. Ah won't slow you down.' He tried to focus but his eyelids flickered with the pain of it. 'Or maybe that's not what's botherin' you.'

Daniel knew what he meant. Charlie. Until he had seen the tears in her eyes, her concern for another man, he hadn't appreciated how much she was starting to mean to him.

'She has that effect,' Al said.

Daniel nodded. 'Let's get going then.'

While Daniel saddled the horses and Charlie bathed Al's face, Al told them what he knew. Besides him, Roy had left five men behind — the old cook, who spent most of his time sleeping, and four others who would be taking it in turns around the clock to guard the hideout.

'Even if we get past the man on the ledge, there'll still be a man somewhere on the outside,' Al said.

'Why would he bother us? We're leaving, not coming,' Charlie said.

Al didn't seem keen to answer, but Daniel already knew the reason. There was no easy way to say it.

'Because Roy left instructions that no one was to leave.'

Al nodded. 'It was more than that.'
'More? What else?' Charlie asked.
'Shoot to kill.'

22

Charlie sat down cross-legged on the ground and hung her head. What she wouldn't give to be dealing with an ornery cowhand, or mending broken-down fences, or even listening to Billy moan about the injustices of life. When did things get so complicated? So dangerous?

'You could have told us that before we saddled the horses,' Daniel said.

'Ah thought you had a plan. Surely you weren't expectin' to just ride out of here?'

Daniel shook his head. 'But I thought we might have a chance against one lookout on the ledge. At the very least, Charlie would have been able to make a break for it.'

'You were going to . . . that's crazy talk. I wouldn't leave you.'

Daniel glanced at Al, but if her

loyalty to another man bothered him, it didn't show on his battered face.

'Well, whatever we do, we need to do it quickly. The mornin' watch will be comin' in soon and this will be their first stop.' Al checked the rounds in his gun and dropped it back in its holster. 'It's going to be them or us.'

'Well whatever we do, we don't want to alert the others,' Charlie opined. 'It needs to be quiet so that we keep the element of surprise.'

Both men nodded their agreement.

'Easier said than done,' Al said. 'Brodie and Bragg are no slouches. They even smell trouble they'll start shootin', and ah don't know how fast you are,' he said addressing Daniel, 'but ah'm no match for either of them.'

'We need a distraction then,' Charlie said. 'Something they don't expect that poses no threat to them.'

'Like ah said, they ain't fools. They'll smell an ambush a mile away. And if they get even a split-second chance, they'll kill Daniel for sure.'

For the next few minutes, they all stood in deep thought. Charlie looked at Al, broken and bruised, then at Daniel, looking little better. Both of them had made sacrifices for her, and would again, she was sure. Yet neither of them were in any shape for a hand-to-hand fight. And neither of them were cold-blooded killers. What chance would they have against the likes of Brodie and Bragg?

'I've got an idea,' she said. 'Do either of you have a spare shirt?'

Both men looked confused, but she held up her hand, rebuffing their questions. If she told them what she was planning, they would only try to stop her and she was already struggling with the idea.

'Just give me a shirt and a few minutes and I'll explain . . . if I need to.'

Daniel looked as if he might suspect when he handed over a shirt he pulled from his saddle-bag, but she turned away quickly and disappeared into a dark corner of the barn before he could comment. Her hands shook as she removed her own shirt and carefully unwound the bindings around her breasts. Quickly, she pulled on Daniel's shirt before slipping off her pants, then released her hair from its tie so that it hung loosely around her face and shoulders.

As she stood tugging at the shirttails, which barely reached halfway down her thighs, she could hardly control the trembling that seemed to physically rock her. Pulling herself together, she retrieved the six-gun that had been tucked down the back of her pants and, holding it behind her back, returned to Al and Daniel.

The ruse worked, and as they gaped at her standing half-naked and dishevelled, she levelled the six-shooter at them.

'That was the distraction I was aiming for,' she said, wondering how the gun wasn't shaking in her hand. 'Do you think it'll work on Brodie and

Bragg, give you enough time to get the drop on them?'

Daniel cleared his throat. 'For sure, if they've got red blood in their veins.'

It was agreed then.

'Are you sure you want to do this?' Al asked.

'No, but we need a distraction,' she said, 'and I don't think either of you wearing just a shirt would have the same effect.'

* * *

From his position hunkered down behind a couple of water barrels, Daniel watched the lookouts ride towards the stable. They were hard-faced men, keen-eyed and watchful. When they reached it, they glanced inside, but there was nothing to see. Al and Charlie had taken their mounts round the back, and there were plenty of dark corners where a person could stand without being immediately obvious.

'Al, you no good Texan — '

Looking ruffled with his shirt hanging half out, and pulling straw out of his hair, Al loped out.

'Is it that time already?'

'You look like Hell. We heard the boss gave you a whooping. I guess one outlaw in the family is enough for him.'

Both men chuckled.

Al grinned. 'If you saw her, you'd know she was worth it.'

Daniel braced himself as Al walked forward to take the horses and lead them away.

'Do you mind pullin' off your own saddles?' Al asked. 'Ah threw my shoulder out again.'

Daniel could only see the men's backs but it was obvious they weren't happy as they followed Al to the corral. He tightened his grip on the Smith & Wesson, but both men did as they were bid, hanging their saddles on the fence while Al released their animals into the empty enclosure.

'You're about as much use as a busted-up chair,' the blonde outlaw complained.

'I think a busted-up chair would be more use,' his short friend added. 'I don't know why the boss keeps him around. Everybody knows the only good Texan is a dead Texan.'

'Maybe we should do Roy a favour and get rid of this bronc-buster along with that other one.'

Apparently, Al believed the threat, and Daniel shifted his weight as he watched Al start to back off. Just then, a noise from inside the stable distracted the newcomers. Before they drew their guns, Charlie wandered out.

'Al, are you going to be much longer? It's getting cold in — '

She stopped, stock still, stammering as though completely caught off guard by the sight of the two men.

'Well, what have we got here?' Shorty [illegible].

Daniel stood up behind them and cocked his gun as Al and Charlie brought their weapons round to bear on the two men.

'What the — '

'Get your hands away from those guns, gents,' Daniel said, moving in closer behind them. 'And don't turn around.'

'Son of a bitch!'

Both men raised their arms to shoulder height, and with a nod to Al and Charlie, Daniel holstered his gun, disarmed the two outlaws and threw their weapons out into the corral. Then, he tied their hands and marched them into the stable, tied their feet, and gagged them. By the time he was finished, Charlie was dressed and Al had the horses waiting. Without a backward glance, they rode out.

After they passed through the trees, they stopped to consider the quarter-mile distance they were going to have to travel across open meadow to reach the tunnel. Daniel couldn't shake the feeling of foreboding that sent a chill through him despite the warmth of the sun on his back.

'You're sure the lookout won't be able to see us?' he asked.

'If he happens to come out back, sure'nuff, but his job is to watch the front,' Al answered.

'I don't see what choice we have,' Charlie said. 'If those two get free, we're done for either way. Come on, let's just go.'

She started her horse forward, and keeping to a steady pace that would minimize the sound of the horses' hoofs, they crossed the meadow. They were within twenty feet of the tunnel when Frank stepped out.

'If you want to make it out of here alive,' he said, covering Daniel with his rifle, 'keep your hand away from that gun.'

23

Daniel rested his hands on the pommel of his saddle. The fact that Frank hadn't already shot him might bode well. Maybe he was worried about hitting Charlie, but Daniel doubted it. The man had already proven himself to be a dead shot, even when outnumbered.

'If?' Daniel asked.

'That's what I said. Now, are you going to try to shoot me, or are you going to listen to what I have to say?'

'I'm listening.'

Frank shifted the rifle into the crook of his arm and looked between the three of them. 'Are you all right, Al? I heard Roy gave you quite a whipping.'

'Ah'm doing all right, Frank. Ah guess whether or not that changes depends on you.'

'You don't need to worry about me,

Al. None of you do. You see, I'm going to step aside and let you go on your way.'

Daniel studied Frank closely, wondering what kind of a poker player he was. His face sure as Hell didn't give away what was going on behind his quiet smile.

'How do we know it's not a trap?' Daniel asked.

'It's a fair question, considering. What do you think, Al?'

'Ah've always found you to be a man of your word, Frank.'

Daniel wasn't convinced. For all he knew, Al could be in on it. 'Why would you just let us pass?'

Frank's stare fixed on him. 'I can shoot you, if that's what you want.'

Charlie pushed Red between them. 'If Al trusts him, I think we have to,' she said, glancing over her shoulder in the direction of the hideout. 'We don't have time for twenty questions.'

Daniel looked back as well. The meadow was empty but there was no guarantee it would stay that way for long.

'That's right, you don't,' Frank said. 'In exactly ten minutes, I'm going to fire off three shots. You know what that means, don't you?'

Daniel nodded, but a question still gnawed at him and he couldn't ignore it. 'Why are you letting us go? We know about the orders Roy left.'

He couldn't bring himself to put them into words. It would be too much like tempting fate.

'Because I don't take my orders from Roy. Never have and never will.'

'Then who are you taking orders from?'

Frank grinned. 'Well, Dan, of course.'

Daniel was puzzled. 'Why would he go against Roy?'

'For the same reason he left you and your ma. To protect you.'

It didn't make sense but the time for talk was over as Frank stepped aside and waved them past.

'Ten minutes,' he said, taking out the

makings and settling down to roll a cigarette.

'You won't mind if I take that rifle and your sidearm,' Daniel said. 'I'll leave them on the other side.'

Frank shrugged and handed them over.

'Ah won't forget this, Frank,' Al said, before heading into the tunnel.

Despite his remaining unease, Daniel brought up the rear keeping a sharp lookout until they were out of sight. He dropped Frank's weapons halfway through. When they emerged at the other end, he had his own gun in hand, but the ledge was deserted. It didn't ease the feeling of being watched, the anticipation that at any moment a bullet would end his life.

Once out in the open, Daniel let Al lead. His knowledge of the terrain was superior to either Daniel or Charlie's and he kept them moving along at a good pace. Nevertheless, it seemed no time at all to Daniel before they heard the three shots.

They were riding single file, strung out as they squeezed between ancient rock falls. His eyes sweeping up the canyon walls could see a dozen places perfect for an ambush.

At the head of the column, Al turned in the saddle and called back, 'If you see anythin' move, just shoot. Blackie Newman's out here somewhere and he's devoted to Roy.'

As he pulled out his Henry rifle, Daniel saw Charlie draw the Yellow Boy from its saddle boot. She glanced back, her face drawn with worry, yet still she managed a grim smile.

When the attack came, Al and Charlie were some way ahead, already spreading out in the canyon where it opened up. As Daniel prepared to catch up to them, a bullet ricocheted close by, and several more kicked up dirt around him. It was obvious the sentry only had one target in mind. Slipping his feet from the stirrups, he ran for the cover of some low boulders.

'You two go on, it's me he's after.'

But it seemed that, without Daniel as a clear target, the gunman was content to divert his attention elsewhere. Charlie's horse reared and, whether by accident or intention, she slid from the saddle and scrambled for cover. Al quickly joined her.

The shooting stopped, probably to let the sentry reload, or maybe he liked the sound of his own voice. 'Hey,' he shouted, 'is that you, Al?'

'Uh huh. And the boss's daughter is with me so be careful where you're shootin'.'

'I don't need to be, if you take her back.'

'I'm not going back,' Charlie shouted.

'Then you better keep your head down, little lady.'

Newman fired a couple of times but there was no way he could get a clear shot at any of them. They could stay there all day, trading bullets, neither side getting anywhere near. Daniel shook his head. That was it. Newman wasn't there to stop him dead. He was there to delay him, give the others time to come up behind and trap him.

He looked around. All three horses had bolted and stood together a hundred yards away looking ready to take flight at the slightest provocation. His eyes wandered the rock-strewn slopes on either side of their position. Scattered scrub oak would provide some cover, a few larger boulders here and there, but cover was sparse if the man ahead was paying attention.

'Al,' Daniel called, keeping his voice as low as possible. 'Can you keep him talking, distract him for a few minutes?'

Al nodded.

'What are you going to do?' Charlie asked.

'I'm going to climb higher, see if I can find a place where I can get a shot at him.'

She nodded and levered a cartridge into the breach of the Yellow Boy. 'Be careful.'

She and Al snapped off a couple of shots.

Keeping in a low crouch, Daniel started his ascent, expecting at any moment to feel the impact of a bullet tearing into his body. Gaining confidence with every foot of ground covered, he climbed higher, sometimes on all fours, sometimes on his belly and at other times in a crouched run.

'Why don't you come down here and talk to us, Mr Newman?' Charlie shouted. 'Maybe we can come to some agreement where no one gets killed.'

'Like you did with Frank? Or did he just let you pass? He always was a Dan man. I told Roy it would be a mistake putting him there.'

Daniel was only half-listening to the conversation going on below him but mention of his father made him pause.

'Frank tried to stop us,' Charlie shouted, 'we just got the better of him.'

'I guess he would have made it seem that way, but I'd bet you 10–1 that Dan told him to let his boy pass.'

'And why would he do that? Only a few days ago he almost killed Daniel himself.'

'Almost? Dan ain't an almost man. If he wanted him dead, he'd be dead.' The sentry fired off a couple of shots. 'Speaking of dead, he ain't, is he?'

Obviously Newman was getting suspicious at his silence, but if Daniel answered he'd give away his position. He started moving, scrambling now where the slope steepened.

'Well?' the sentry asked when his enquiry was greeted with silence.

'I'm alive, just waiting for you to shut up long enough for me to get a word in.'

Daniel did a double take. Surely that wasn't . . . but who else was there except the Texan? Charlie certainly couldn't have disguised her voice so effectively. He grinned. There was more to that bronc-buster than met the eye. The man was a natural mimic, maybe too good for Daniel's liking.

'It's good to hear your voice,' the

sentry shouted. 'There's a hundred dollars for whichever one of us takes you down.'

Newman sounded close now, and choosing a flat boulder to kneel behind, Daniel sighted across the slope to where the sound of his voice seemed to be coming from. Below him, Charlie had resumed her verbal bombardment, reasoning but not pleading with Newman to let them pass.

Clever girl, he thought.

Every exchange demanded a response from the sentry, thereby helping Daniel to pinpoint his location. After only a few minutes, Daniel spotted him downslope, a swarthy man dressed in a light-coloured shirt, pressed in behind a split boulder about a hundred yards away.

Daniel brought the Henry rifle up and, after wiping the sweat away from his eyes, carefully took aim and fired. The shot took the guard in the arm and as he whirled around to return fire,

Daniel shot him again in the chest. He collapsed, dead or dying, Daniel couldn't tell, but definitely without the strength to fight on as the rifle fell from his outstretched hand.

With a quick look towards their back trail, and seeing no one, Daniel made his way back down the slope. It was much quicker than his ascent, mainly a slide down on his backside and elbows.

Al had already caught the horses by the time Daniel planted his feet on level ground.

'Is he dead?' Charlie asked.

Daniel nodded. 'But we need to go. He was just there to slow us down. Once Brodie and Bragg get loose they'll be right behind us.'

She nodded and fired off three, evenly spaced shots. 'Maybe that will stall them.'

* * *

The afternoon sun was starting to cool and fade before they heard the thunder of hoofs. They had just reached the bottom of a series of switchbacks, visible against the canyon wall like a zigzag staircase. No more than 500 yards from top to bottom, but each section was a narrow ledge, wide enough for one horse. There was no shelter and no turning back once they started.

'This isn't the way we came,' Charlie said.

'This is a short cut. Not so many people know about it,' Al assured her. 'There'll be less chance of us runnin' into any more trouble.'

'Is it safe?'

'It'll be difficult but nothing we can't handle.'

Charlie looked doubtful.

'From bottom to top we're going to be sitting ducks to anyone coming around that bend,' Daniel said.

Al nodded. 'Ah thought about that. We're goin' to have to make a stand here.'

'You don't think we can make it

before they reach us?' Charlie asked.

Both men shook their heads.

'You should go ahead though, Charlie,' Daniel said, pushing her hat back so that her hair flowed freely about her face and shoulders. 'If they see it's you, they won't shoot. If they get past us, at least you'll have a head start.'

'Is that what you think I should do, Al?' she asked.

'Yes, darlin', I do.'

'But you know I'm a good shot. Don't you think I can help?'

'Ah know that. You could probably shoot both of those fellers off their horses before they knew what was happenin', but you're not a killer.' Al chuckled. 'Besides, the trail's only wide enough for one rider at a time. You might as well show Daniel here how it's done.'

Daniel didn't take offence. Al was trying to reassure her and he couldn't blame him for that, especially when he saw her face change from mild indignation to reluctant acceptance.

'All right,' she said, starting the horse forward, 'but I'll be waiting for you at the top, both of you, so don't disappoint me.'

Without further ado, Daniel and Al secured their horses and took up positions behind a rockslide. The location gave them an unhindered view of the bend where the riders would have to emerge, and they agreed that as soon as they saw them they would open fire. Al assured Daniel they had no choice. Brodie and Bragg would be out for blood.

Minutes dragged by. The sound of hoofs quieted with the riders slowing down their approach. Loose rocks tumbled down the canyon wall behind them and Daniel ventured a look up. Charlie was about halfway, pressing on without a backward glance, using all her skill and concentration to manoeuvre Red up the narrow trail.

The sound of the pursuing riders quieted to an eerie silence.

'Here they come,' Al said. 'Keep your

eyes open. Remember, they won't hesitate to kill us.'

Sweat trickled down Daniel's temple. He wanted to wipe it away but he didn't dare move, didn't dare break his concentration. His eyes scanned the walls either side of the bend, looking for movement, but there was nothing to see.

Time passed slowly, marked only by the lengthening shadows that darkened the canyon walls. The longer they waited, the more dangerous it became. With the light fading, shadows became hiding places where a man could slip into position unseen.

'Do you see anything?' Daniel asked.

'No, but they're out there.'

Just then a slight movement, no more than a trickle of gravel, caught Daniel's eye about fifty yards ahead up in the rocks. He glimpsed colour and opened fire without hesitation. The blonde outlaw staggered and fell, clutching at his chest. Rolling onto the trail below, he lay still.

Immediately, shots from the opposite side of the bend hit near their position. Daniel felt his cheek sting as a spray of rock slivers opened up the skin below his eye. Before he could lever another cartridge into the breach, Al was returning fire. But the second outlaw was in a better position than his friend had been and none of the shots found their target.

'This is pointless,' Daniel said when Al stopped to reload. 'He can't see us, we can't see him.'

'You're right. Do you know what we need?'

'Luck.'

Al shook his head and grinned. 'A stick of dynamite.'

Keeping low, he ran across to his horse and pulled off the saddle-bags. Bringing them back, he looked in one and then the other, eventually bringing out a coil of fuse, and a cylindrical tube about seven inches long, wrapped in waxy paper.

'That's dynamite?' Daniel asked,

never having seen it before.

'Uh-huh.'

Daniel watched Al deftly slice off six inches from the fuse and throw it away.

'Do you know what you're doing with that?'

Al cut off a fresh six inches, poking the end of the fuse into the dynamite, which he then squeezed tightly.

'Ah sure hope so, otherwise we'll be the ones going bang. Do you have a match?'

Although he didn't smoke, Daniel always carried a small box in his pocket. He handed it over, feeling somewhat intrigued as to why the bronc-buster would have dynamite in his saddle-bags.

As if reading his mind, Al said, 'Roy got hold of some for the job they're on and ah thought it might come in handy.' He struck a match. 'Get ready.'

There was a hiss when he set it alight, sparks flying as the flame devoured the fuse. With a mighty heave, he lobbed it to the place where the gunman had last been. There was a slight delay between it hitting the ground and the explosion. Simultaneously, the gunman stood up and flung himself away as dirt and rock sprayed everywhere.

Daniel fired off a couple of opportunistic shots and heard him scream.

'Let's get out of here,' Daniel said, running for his horse.

24

Above them, Charlie had a good view from the canyon rim. Any other time, she would have enjoyed watching the changing landscape as the sun prepared to set. But now her gaze shifted between the men on the ground and her friends who were steadily climbing the canyon wall. Brodie and Bragg appeared to be dead. They certainly hadn't moved since the dust cleared. Nonetheless, she held the Yellow Boy ready, prepared to shoot if she perceived any threat.

She waited. She watched. Down on the canyon floor, nothing stirred. Carrion birds circled overhead, eyeing the pickings below. As Al and Daniel made their way slowly up the trail, she could hear the sound of the horses' hoofs over the uneven terrain, a few words spoken in encouragement.

She noticed Al had fallen behind. The mare he was riding was skittish and it seemed to be taking all his strength to hold the animal as it fought to find its own way. She saw him stop, stroking its neck as he leaned forward and spoke into its ear. It seemed to help. The little mare stood quietly as Al stretched his back and rolled his shoulders tentatively. He looked up at Charlie, his expression strained.

'Be careful, Al,' she called.

He nodded, lightly touching his heels to the mare. The animal moved on warily, showing the whites of its eyes.

They were nearing the top when Daniel's horse faltered. She saw him tighten the reins, overcompensating as the horse moved sideways, perilously close to the edge. For a moment the grey stopped, pawing and stamping the ground with its front legs.

'Steady,' Charlie cautioned under her breath.

They moved on as the edge of the path crumbled, sending loose dirt and rocks falling away. Below them, the little mare panicked as the debris showered it. In a frenzy, it tried to turn and despite Al's best efforts, horse and rider plunged off the trail and down into the canyon.

Charlie closed her eyes. After everything they had been through, to lose Al now was inconceivable. She couldn't bear to have her worst fears confirmed.

She flinched when Daniel grabbed her arm, pulling her back from the edge.

'Don't look,' he cautioned.

'Is he . . . ?'

Daniel nodded.

It wasn't that she didn't believe him, but she needed to see for herself. Moving tentatively to the edge, she looked over. Horse and rider lay twisted and unmoving at the bottom.

'Al?' she shouted.

Daniel dragged her back. 'He's dead, Charlie. Nobody could survive a fall like that. Not even Al.'

She knew he was right but it didn't

make acceptance any easier. 'We should at least go down there and bury him.'

'We should, but it's too dangerous. We're already losing the light. One false step and we'd be down there with him. He wouldn't want that.'

She couldn't argue with his reasoning, although she wanted to. Al didn't deserve to die like that, then to be left like a piece of meat for the buzzards to feast on. She wanted to scream, to argue about the injustice of it all, but what would be the point? Nothing would bring him back.

'I'm done with it all,' she said, catching up the reins of her waiting horse. 'When we find a town, I'll pay you what I owe you and we can go our separate ways.'

25

Brunton — six weeks later

The bell above the door tinkled when Charlie pushed her way into the telegraph office. Behind the low counter, the operator made a few taps on his equipment then looked up and smiled broadly.

'Good afternoon, Miss Wells. How are you today?'

'I'm well, Mr Wilson. How are you?'

It was the same greeting they had exchanged every day since she had arrived in Brunton. He didn't wait for her next question since it was always the same. Instead he took a slip of paper from a pile on the desk and handed it to her.

'This came for you a few minutes ago. I was going to bring it over later if . . . '

She read it then slipped it into the

small bag hanging from her wrist. 'Thank you. Good day.'

'Miss Wells?'

She stopped, waiting as Mr Wilson hurried round his desk. He was a tall man, around thirty years of age, always neat and tidy in his appearance, impeccable in his manners. His breath smelled of mint.

'Yes?'

There was a sheen on his upper lip and he looked a little flustered. 'I was wondering if you'd have supper with me this evening. Nothing fancy, you understand, just a meal between . . . erm . . . friends?'

Friends. It was an interesting choice of word and instantly off-putting.

'I'm busy. Maybe another time.'

His shoulders sagged, the light in his puppy dog brown eyes dimming despite the forced smile that remained on his lips. 'Of course. Let me get the door for you.'

She didn't look back as she crossed the busy street, although she was sure he would be watching. That he wanted to be more than friends hadn't escaped her attention. Her landlady at the boarding house, Mrs Brown, never missed an opportunity to tell her how much her nephew, Mr Wilson, admired her favourite boarder.

She stepped up onto the plank walk, nodding politely to a couple of ladies who passed by arm-in-arm, then to a man who stepped aside and tipped his Derby hat to her. Further along, Mrs Brown exited the bank and waved before heading off in the opposite direction, much to Charlie's relief.

Reluctant to catch up with the woman, Charlie stopped to look in a store window, but it was her own reflection that caught her eye. Wearing a plain blue dress, high at the neck and long in the sleeve, her hair combed and tied at the back with a ribbon, she was as much a stranger to herself as she was to these folks. She sighed, unhappily. What would they say, she wondered, if they knew the truth about Charlotte Wells?

* * *

Further along Main Street, Daniel looked up from his hammering and wiped sweat from his brow. Up on the unfinished roof of what was to be the new hospital, the sun beat down relentlessly, but the high vantage point gave him a rewarding view of the growing town. He took a swig of water from his canteen, letting his gaze roam as he swilled the cooling liquid around his mouth before swallowing.

Even in a town like this it was easy to spot newcomers. Men riding tired horses, their eyes scanning the street for the nearest saloon. Salesmen who came in by stage or train, carrying heavy cases from business to business. Covered wagons driven by weary travellers, trundling along to the land office.

But it was none of these that caught his eye today. Hanging his hammer over a beam, he climbed down. 'I'm going to get something to eat,' he shouted to a man bent over a table looking at plans.

The man raised his hand without looking up and Daniel strode away down the street.

'Charlie.'

She turned around with a start and he caught her elbow to steady her. For a split second, he thought she was going to hit him, but then she smiled.

'Daniel, it's been a while. How long have you been back in town?'

'A couple of days. I'm working down the street and I thought it was you.' He chuckled as he looked her over. 'I still can't get used to you in a dress.'

'Me neither,' she said, unenthusiastically.

'I was just on my way to Sadie May's for something to eat.' He offered her his arm. 'Care to join me?'

She hooked her arm through his and together they walked the short distance to the cafe. It was starting to fill up with the midday rush but Sadie May quickly found them a table at the back. Daniel knew she was sweet on him and her indignation at seeing Charlie on his arm didn't go unnoticed. When his piece of pie arrived it was much smaller than usual.

'I hear you've been giving riding lessons to some of the kids in town,' Daniel said, finishing his last bite.

'Only a couple of times a week. It gives me something to do, and it's good for Red. I ride him every morning but he misses the outdoors, the freedom.'

Daniel sensed the admission was as much about her as the horse. He noticed she looked pale, her tan all but gone, and she had gained weight. Not much, and he liked the curves that gently filled out her dress in all the right places. What he didn't like was the listlessness, the dullness in her eyes, the down turned corners of her mouth.

Sadie May brought more coffee but didn't offer seconds on the pie the way she usually did. She barely glanced at Charlie.

'I heard from the lawyer today,' Charlie said, breaking the silence that had settled between them. 'He's coming into town in a couple of days to finalize my uncle's will.'

'That's good news. What will you do then?'

She pondered the question. 'I thought about buying a small ranch. It's what I know, but after what happened to the Crooked-W, I'm not sure I want the responsibility.'

'I could make some enquiries. This town's full of opportunities if you know who to talk to.'

She shook her head. 'I wouldn't stay here.'

'You wouldn't? Where would you go?'

She looked uncomfortable. Uncharacteristically, she lowered her gaze. 'Somewhere that nobody knows me.' She got up abruptly. 'Thank you for the pie, Daniel. It's been nice seeing you again. Take care of yourself. Goodbye.'

He watched her leave, knowing it was pointless trying to stop her. And what right did he have to try anyway? Before they had arrived in Brunton she had made it clear that she wanted a fresh start, to sever all ties with the past, and he had agreed, assuming that their friendship would be exempt.

But now, with a simple goodbye, he realized it wasn't. He had extended the hand of friendship and she had refused it. Maybe she was right. Maybe it was time for them both to move on.

26

'Good job, Mr Smith,' the stationmaster said, standing back to admire the black and gold painted sign that now adorned the platform wall and elegantly announced the arrival of train passengers to Brunton. 'You are indeed a craftsman, sir.'

'It just takes a steady hand.' Daniel picked up his tool bag. 'If you need anything else doing, just speak to Mr Morgan.'

'I certainly will. In fact, I was wondering if you might . . . ' He tilted his ear to listen into the distance. 'That sounds like the 1.30 train rolling in. Do you mind waiting a few minutes? There's a pot of coffee on the stove inside, if you want to help yourself.'

He hurried away, putting on his stationmaster's hat as he went, while Daniel accepted his offer and went inside. After looking around the office and seeing nothing of particular interest to him, Daniel moved to the window where he could see the passengers disembarking.

He hadn't travelled on a train but it looked agreeable. The people were clean and seemed to be rested, a far cry from the film of dust, and the aches and pains that accompanied a stage ride. He had tried that once and it didn't suit him, being cooped up in a small space with a bunch of strangers, being bumped and jostled.

As the last of the passengers stepped down and the platform started to clear, Daniel finished his coffee and put his cup on the desk. Stepping outside, he almost collided with a man carrying a saddle. He dropped his tools, bending quickly to retrieve them, mildly annoyed with the man's ignorance when he walked on without a word of apology.

Looking around for the stationmaster, Daniel couldn't see him. Well, whatever it was he wanted he would have to see Morgan about it another time, Daniel decided. Today was his last day as a carpenter, and he had one more job to do. The sooner that was done, the sooner he could collect his pay and leave town.

As he left the station, he noticed the man with the saddle. He appeared to be looking in the window of a ladies' haberdashery, but as Daniel approached, he turned and looked him full in the face. The saddle dropped to the ground, freeing up his only arm.

'Fancy seeing you here,' Ralph Stanton said. 'I wondered if you'd still be with the girl.' He grinned. 'No need to deny it. I followed that lawyer of hers. He led me straight here.'

Daniel wished he was wearing his gun, but Brunton was at least half civilized and after a few weeks in town he had seen no need for it while he was working.

'What are you doing here?' he asked, forgoing any small talk.

'I'm here to collect a bounty, two now, it turns out.'

Daniel's confusion must have shown.

'You haven't heard? Val Johnson's put a bounty on your heads, five hundred dollars apiece on you and that girl.'

'Why?'

'For what you did to Scott.'

'It was a fair fight. He deserved it.'

Stanton shrugged as if he didn't care. 'Doc said that beating you gave him damaged his brain. He ain't spoke a word since he woke up. Ain't able to walk unless somebody helps him. Can't even feed himself properly most days. It's pitiful. You should have just killed him.'

He studied Daniel's expression, his eyes narrowing.

'But I don't think it was you that did it. It was the girl. The boss didn't like that idea but he had a feeling stoving a man's head in wasn't your style. Well, it makes no never mind to me. You were both there and the boy's worse off than dead. The bounty's payable on one or both of you and I ain't got no worries about collecting.'

Daniel held up his hands. 'I'm unarmed. If you gun me down here, it'll be murder. A private bounty issued by Val Johnson won't hold water with a judge.'

'Kill an unarmed man? The thought never crossed my mind.' He chuckled mirthlessly. 'No, not for a second. In fact, I'm willing to bet you'll be wearing that Smith & Wesson of yours within the hour and I can wait.'

Ralph Stanton tipped his hat to a passing lady then picked up his saddle. He brushed past Daniel and stepped to the edge of the plank walk, stopping to let a wagon roll by.

'Looks like that lawyer's on the move,' he remarked. 'Where do you think he's going in such an all-fired hurry? Maybe I'll just follow him, see where he leads me.'

A chill ran down Daniel's spine. He grabbed Stanton by the shoulder, knocking him off balance. The saddle landed in the dirt with a thud, drawing the attention of several passers-by, including a man wearing a deputy's badge.

'Have we got some trouble here, gents?' the lawdog asked, moving in closer.

'I lost my balance. You'd be surprised how much difference that arm made,' Stanton said, looking towards his empty sleeve. 'This feller was just helping me.'

The deputy picked up Stanton's saddle and handed it to him. 'I hope that's all it was. I wouldn't like to see either of you gents in a cell for disturbing the peace.'

27

Lawyer Malcolm Enright was younger than Charlie expected. Probably only in his middle thirties, short in stature with a thick head of dark hair, and keen blue eyes, a good-looking man. When he shook her hand, his grasp was confident without being overbearing, and immediately put her at her ease.

'Miss Wells, it's a pleasure to meet you at last.' He smiled. 'I'm Malcolm Enright Junior. Unfortunately, my father isn't in good health so he asked me to come in his stead. However, I can assure you of the same care and attention he would have given you. That said, I'm hoping we can conclude our business today so that I can be on the train back this evening.'

Mrs Brown brought a tray into the boarding house dining room and carefully deposited a coffee pot and two cups before Charlie and her guest.

Enright waited for her to leave before continuing. 'Your uncle's will was straightforward. As you know, everything reverts to you.' He handed her a page of figures. 'There wasn't a lot in the way of cash, around two thousand dollars after we deducted the advance we sent you and took our fees, but the land and cattle will have value.'

Charlie passed him a cup of coffee. 'Would have if I still had possession, you mean.'

Enright didn't seem to have an answer to that and she hadn't expected one. For several minutes they sat in silence, Charlie looking blankly at the page in front of her while Enright searched for something in his case. Finally, Enright finished his paper-shuffling and cleared his throat.

'I should tell you that there has been an enquiry regarding the Crooked-W.'

'Enquiry?'

'A party interested in buying the land and whatever stock can be . . . salvaged.

Of course the offer was for a fraction of what it's worth but — '

'Who made the offer?'

'The buyer asked to remain anonymous.'

'I bet he did,' she said, immediately thinking of Val Johnson.

It would be just like him to make a legitimate offer. What had her Uncle Tom called him? A businessman. She shrugged off her growing anger as best she could.

'Whatever the offer is, unless I know who I'm dealing with, I'm not interested.'

Despite her best effort, it was hard to control her resentment and she regretted her tone as Enright fumbled around in his case again.

'I'll see what I can do,' he said, handing her a pen and an inkpot. 'If I can just get your signature on a couple of documents, I can release the money to you immediately, in cash, as you requested. I'm sure any other business regarding the sale of the ranch can be dealt with at a later date.'

After indicating where he required her signature, he handed her a copy of the documents and an envelope. She didn't count the money. As he prepared to leave, he seemed to remember something.

'By the way, your father contacted us. He wanted to know your whereabouts but as per your instructions we declined his request.'

'Was he contesting the details of the will?'

'No, not at all. He made it quite clear that as previously set out by Mr Mason and himself, all land and assets were to go directly to you in the event of your marriage or Mr Mason's death.'

'Did he say what he wanted?'

'Not directly, but if I was to hazard a guess, I'd say he was concerned about your welfare.'

Charlie resisted the urge to laugh. 'Well, if he contacts you again, you can tell him that my welfare is no concern of his.'

The lawyer looked puzzled but merely nodded and said, 'As you wish, Miss Wells.'

As he stood up to leave, Mrs Brown appeared at the door, looking red-faced and annoyed.

'Sorry to interrupt you, but there's another gentleman here to see you, Miss Wells.' She placed particular emphasis on the word gentleman.

'Mr Enright was just leaving.'

'I'll show him out then,' Mrs Brown said abruptly, ushering the lawyer towards the front of the house. 'Your other visitor is waiting for you in the yard.' Before she passed, she leaned in close and lowered her voice. 'And I'd appreciate it if that's where he stays. I try not to judge but I draw the line at having gunmen in my home.'

28

Charlie peered out of the kitchen window before going to the door. She could think of several gunmen, none of whom she wanted to see. The small yard appeared to be empty, although the gate swung freely on its creaky hinges.

She pressed her face close to the glass and glimpsed a man's shoulder. He was standing outside the door and, as she watched, she heard him try the handle. Glancing to her right, she saw the key wobble in the lock but the door stayed put.

He stepped back and stared towards the window and the hard knot of foreboding in Charlie's stomach softened. Quickly, she went outside, closing the door behind her as Mrs Brown entered the kitchen. A glance at the Smith & Wesson worn low on Daniel's hip and tied at the thigh warned her something wasn't right.

'What's wrong?'

'We've got trouble.'

Quickly, he told her about his conversation with Ralph Stanton. With each detail, she felt herself getting panicky.

'It's never going to be over now,' she said, when he finished. 'Wherever we go, somebody is always going to be looking for us. Johnson. My pa. The Lord only knows how many other people we've crossed along the way.'

He didn't comment. He didn't need to. His taut expression said it all. There was never going to be any peace for them now that Johnson had put a price on their heads.

'Sounds like quite the dilemma,' a new voice said.

Charlie had never seen Ralph Stanton but she knew instinctively that this was him. He wasn't big or ugly or scarred in any way, except for his missing arm. His clothes were relatively clean and fitted well. Even the empty sleeve of his jacket was carefully tucked in and pinned at the shoulder. Leaning idly against the corner of the boarding house, a casual observer wouldn't have given him a second look.

But looking into his pale, soulless eyes, Charlie felt her insides quiver.

* * *

Daniel felt himself go cold inside.

'I see you strapped on your gun,' Stanton said, straightening up and shoving his jacket back behind his holster. 'I guess there's no time like the present.'

So this was it. Kill or be killed. Killed most likely. Stanton was good. Not just fast, but good. His reputation included the boast that he never needed more than one bullet to kill a man.

It would take a miracle for Daniel to come out of this alive.

'When you're ready, time's awastin',' Stanton said, goading him.

Daniel wondered if he would even

get his gun out before Stanton's bullet finished him. If only there was some way he could slow him down, a split second distraction, then at least he might get one shot off. An idea crossed his mind. It was a long shot but if he was going to die, his last thought would at least be a pleasant one.

He cleared his throat. 'Did you ever see a pretty girl wearing only a man's shirt?'

There was no time to wait and see if the remark had done its job. Daniel drew and fired, turning aside in one fluid movement. Stanton's gun had come out of its holster, but blood was already starting to appear on the front of his shirt. When Daniel's second bullet hit him, Stanton's shot went high.

Inside the boarding house, Mrs Brown screamed. Outside on the street, the sound of running feet heralded the arrival of several citizens, amongst them the deputy whom Daniel had seen earlier.

Quickly, Daniel slid his smoking gun

back into its holster.

'Care to tell me what just happened here?' the deputy asked, sticking a toe into Stanton's corpse.

'That's Ralph Stanton,' Daniel murmured, staring at the corpse. 'He's wanted for armed robbery and murder.'

A collective gasp went up from the small crowd.

The deputy eyed Daniel with suspicion. 'Are you a bounty hunter?'

Daniel shook his head.

'Have you got any proof that any of what you're saying is true?'

Charlie stepped forward. 'If you check your wanted posters, I'm sure you'll find one with his face on it. There probably aren't many outlaws with one arm missing.'

The deputy frowned. 'Well, until I can check that out, I need your friend to surrender his gun and follow me.'

The lawman held out his hand and Daniel handed over his weapon without offering any resistance.

'Am I under arrest?' he asked, as the

deputy took his arm and pushed him between the bystanders.

'That's for the marshal to decide.'

* * *

Daniel was relieved when they didn't throw him in a cell. Instead he was shown to a bench that stood against a wall with a notice board displaying a dozen or more wanted posters. The deputy stood close by, his hand near his holstered gun.

Charlie was given a seat in front of the marshal's desk. She sat tall and straight, her expression impassive, her gaze down turned to her hands folded in her lap.

'Daniel Smith, you say.' Marshal Don Pride leaned his elbows on his desk and regarded Daniel over steepled fingers. 'I don't know the name but I know your face.'

Daniel tried to remain impassive.

'You work for Barlow Morgan, don't you?'

He allowed himself to breathe. 'That's right.'

'I heard him mention you a couple of times. He says you're a hard worker, skilled at what you do. Are you a carpenter by trade, Mr Smith?'

Daniel nodded. It seemed as good a trade as any, far removed from being a gunfighter at least.

'And who are you, miss?' the marshal asked, switching his attention with only the movement of his eyes.

Charlie's head came up slowly, her steady gaze meeting the marshal's. His eyes flickered and he shifted position, leaning back in his chair, arms folded across his chest.

'Charlotte Wells. I board with Mrs Brown. Mr Smith and I came into town together.'

'And what's your relationship to Mr Smith?'

'Family friends.'

The marshal's eyes narrowed, his gaze moving thoughtfully between Charlie and Daniel. 'And what brings you to Brunton?' he asked, adding, 'If you don't mind my asking?'

She didn't hesitate. 'My uncle and cousin were recently killed, our ranch was taken over and I was forced to leave my home.'

Her candour seemed to unsettle the burly marshal even more than her unflinching gaze. And Daniel had no doubt that was Charlie's intention. He could hear it in her voice, see it in her bearing. She was facing him down.

'I'm sorry to hear that,' he said, his tone softening. 'Do you have family in Brunton?'

'No. My lawyer, Mr Enright, suggested we meet here. If you need to check any of what I've told you, he'll be at the hotel until his train leaves tonight.'

'I'll do that.'

The marshal unholstered his Colt and placed it on the desk near his hand then nodded to his deputy. 'See what Mr Enright has to say.'

The deputy nodded and left.

'So, Mr Smith,' the marshal continued, 'tell me how a carpenter came to be in a gunfight with Ralph Stanton and lived to tell?'

Daniel kept it simple, following Charlie's lead and keeping as close to the truth as possible. He explained how he had recognized Stanton as one of the men involved in the murder of Charlie's family. He had seen Stanton following Mr Enright and had confronted him. Stanton had stated that he intended to do Charlie harm. Daniel had duly gone to warn Charlie and that's when Stanton had shown up.

'And you got the drop on him. I'd like to have seen that,' the marshal said. 'I witnessed Stanton kill a man in Tucson a few years back. He was as good as his reputation. What does that make you?'

Daniel shrugged. 'Lucky?'

'Seems so.'

He asked a few more general questions while they waited for the deputy to return. An hour later, satisfied with the validity of their story as supported by the lawyer, he handed the Smith & Wesson back to Daniel.

'There won't be any charges . . . this time,' he said. 'Stanton was a dangerous wanted criminal. It seems to me, based on what you've both told me, that you were just doing your civic duty. I'll see to it that you get any reward that's due.'

He held out his hand and he and Daniel shook on it before he showed them out.

'By the way, my deputy ran into Morgan on his way to see the lawyer. Morgan mentioned that you were thinking about leaving town. I think under the circumstances that would be a good idea.'

Cordially, the marshal tipped his hat to Charlie then closed the door on them.

'Did he just tell me to get out of town?' Daniel asked.

'It sounded like it. And I don't think it's a bad idea. Stanton found us and chances are he won't be the only one showing up to collect those bounties.'

That thought and more had already crossed Daniel's mind. Now that he had killed Stanton, anyone else hoping to claim the bounty would be wary of him. There'd be no chance for any more lucky shots.

He looked around at the busy street. 'We can't stay here,' he said, slipping her hand through the crook of his arm. 'How about I walk you back to the boarding house?'

'Then what?'

He hesitated. 'We have to decide what we're going to do next.'

29

When they arrived at the boarding house, they agreed to meet later that evening and Charlie entered through the front entrance. She couldn't face the yard, even though the body would have been removed by now. More importantly, she didn't feel like talking to Mrs Brown, who would be in the kitchen fussing over something or other.

The hallway was empty and quickly and quietly she made her way upstairs. As she approached her room, she noticed that the door was ajar. She stopped to listen. The house was unusually quiet, not even the sound of pots and pans rattling in the kitchen below.

Easing her way along the landing, she peered in through the narrow gap, listening for any sound that might betray an intruder. But nothing stirred and everything looked to be in its place. She pushed the door open, pausing before she went inside.

Now that she could see more clearly, she decided someone had been there. The top drawer of the dresser was slightly open. The patchwork quilt that covered the bed was rumpled, as if someone had sat down then forgotten to straighten it. Checking inside the armoire, she noticed her saddle-bags and boots had been moved.

Crossing to the dresser, she opened the bottom drawer where her range clothes were washed and folded. Here too, there were signs of rummaging. Reaching her hand between the layers of clothing, her fingers found the Yellow Boy and then her old pistol. Leaving the rifle, she pulled out the gun and checked the chambers. It was loaded, cleaned and oiled, exactly the way she had left it.

'Are they really yours?'

Mrs Brown stood in the doorway, arms folded across her bosom, looking pale and disturbed. Her eyes were red-rimmed, as if she had been crying, and her tone lacked its usual good-natured motherly bluster.

Charlie nodded.

'I want you out of my house today,' Mrs Brown stated. 'Get your things and go.'

'What happened earlier, it wasn't — '

The landlady held up her hand, shaking her head constantly. 'Wasn't your fault? Maybe that's true but you brought a killer to my home. You brought guns into my home. I can't have that. I won't.'

Charlie decided not to argue. The woman was already close to hysteria. Instead, she walked purposefully across the room, feeling a sense of sadness when Mrs Brown backed away.

'I'll be gone in fifteen minutes,' she said, shutting the door.

* * *

She emerged onto the street ten minutes later, saddle-bags thrown over one shoulder, her coat draped across the other to hide the presence of the Yellow Boy to any but the most curious observer. She had an hour to kill until Daniel was due to fetch her, but feeling Mrs Brown's glare boring into her back, she decided not to wait around.

Keeping mainly to the back streets to avoid questioning stares, she made her way towards the livery stable. After a few words with the old hostler, she left her belongings in Red's stall, hiding the Yellow Boy under an old blanket and a layer of straw. The six-gun she dropped into her coat pocket before heading out onto Main Street.

The sun had faded, the sky turning prematurely dark with the threat of rain filling the air. She looked one way and then the other, wondering where Daniel might be. He had mentioned paying a visit to Bulow Morgan to collect the balance of his wages. If her memory served, the builder had an office in the centre of town, not far from Sadie May's eatery.

When she arrived, a middle-aged man looked up from his work at a large drawing board and told her that Daniel had been and gone. That had been fifteen minutes ago and he thought he had heard him mention Bolger's store.

The bell above the door tinkled pleasantly when she entered Bolger's. Behind the long counter, a young man with his shirtsleeves rolled up to the elbow and wearing an apron looked up from some figures he was tallying.

He smiled. 'Good afternoon. How can I help you?'

'I'm looking for someone. I was told he might be here.'

She looked around the spacious room, stocked with every kind of ware from flour to shirts. Floor-to-ceiling shelves filled the walls with no space left empty. There was no sign of Daniel.

'It looks like I missed him.'

'Could I ask the gentleman's name?

Perhaps I could redirect you,' he offered, pleasantly.

'Smith.'

'You're in luck.' He placed his hand on the burlap sack next to him. 'I've just finished getting Mr Smith's order ready and he should be back any minute to collect it.'

Just then, the bell tinkled and Daniel hurried inside. He pushed Charlie towards the counter.

'How much do I owe you?' he asked the clerk, his gaze straying back to the door.

'Seven dollars and forty-five cents, if you please.'

Daniel handed over the money and grabbed up the sack. 'Is there a back door out of here?'

The clerk looked startled but when Daniel grabbed Charlie by the arm and started leading her towards the back of the store, he hurried ahead of them. After taking them through a small office, he unbolted a back door and waved them out into a covered yard.

Inside the store, the bell above the door tinkled.

'Don't go back inside,' Daniel told him. 'Go around the front, wait for them to leave. Fetch the marshal if you want.'

With his fingers biting into her arm, Charlie followed Daniel out of the yard and into an alley that ran along behind several business premises before opening out onto Main Street.

'Who were they?' she asked.

'Nobody I recognized.'

'Then why are we running?'

'Because they've been following us since we left the marshal's office. If they wanted to ask the time, I think they would have done it by now.'

'Following us?' She stumbled, but he dragged her on. 'I didn't see anyone when I left the boarding house.'

He slowed to a walk, holding her back before they emerged onto Main Street. Peering over his shoulder, Charlie didn't see anything out of the ordinary. Of the people still on the street, most were either finishing up their business for the day in preparation for heading home or were already on their way there.

'We need to get off the street,' Daniel said, pushing her back against the wall.

'And go where?'

He thought about it for a minute. 'Sadie May's. The marshal eats there most evenings, so we should be safe enough for now.'

When they arrived, most of the tables were empty. It was still early and the supper crowd hadn't started arriving yet. Daniel's prediction had been right and the marshal was already there, bent over a plate of steak and potatoes, reading a newssheet. He glanced up when they entered, his eyes narrowing as he looked them over.

With a deferential nod, they passed him and took up a table at the back of the room, waiting until Sadie May had taken their order before putting their heads together.

'So, what happened?' Daniel asked.

'Why didn't you stay at the boarding house like we agreed?'

'Mrs Brown threw me out.' Briefly she explained what had happened. 'So I took my gear down to the livery stable and came looking for you.'

Daniel shook his head, his disapproval obvious.

'I didn't see anybody following me,' she said, feeling the need to justify herself. 'Do you think they're working for Johnson?'

'Impossible to say. For all I know, they just wanted to get a look at the man that killed Ralph Stanton.'

He rubbed his eyes, snaking his hand around to massage the back of his neck.

'Probably,' she said, wanting to ease some of the tension. 'But I think you were right to be careful. I should have been, but I just didn't think.'

He didn't comment, although his tight-lipped expression said he didn't disagree. They sat quietly for a few minutes until Sadie May brought out two plates of food. Charlie noticed the woman's hand trembled when she placed Daniel's plate in front of him.

'Long day?' Daniel asked her.

Sadie May concentrated on folding the cloth she had used to carry the hot plates, avoiding eye contact.

'Same as usual,' she said. 'Can I get you anything else?'

'No, thanks.'

Without another word or a glance, she scurried away.

'Word's obviously getting around. Where are you going to stay tonight?' Daniel asked.

'I'll take a room at the hotel.'

He frowned, but again didn't offer any comment as he bit into a chunk of steak.

'You don't think that's a good idea?'

He shrugged and carried on eating but Charlie pushed her plate away, losing her appetite as her confidence faltered. Something about him was different, although it was hard to read him these days. Since they had arrived in town, he had kept his distance. Maybe, he didn't want to be saddled with her anymore. If that was the case, she certainly wouldn't blame him.

'What will you do?' she asked, fearing his answer. 'Take the marshal's advice and leave town?'

He dropped his fork, bumping the table as he got to his feet. 'I know you wanted to go your own way — '

'That's not what I wanted. I just needed — '

'And I respected that, but things are different now. Until we know what those two want, it'll be safer if we stay together so I'll fetch my gear and move over to the hotel tonight.'

She started to stand but he pressed her back down.

'You stay here. This place is starting to fill up and the marshal hasn't started on his second piece of pie yet. Whoever they are, they won't try anything in a crowd.'

She grabbed his hand. 'Be careful, Daniel. I've lost too many people I care about already. I don't want to add you to the list.'

30

Charlie pushed food around her plate while she waited. Several men entered, taking their seats without even glancing in her direction. The marshal finished his pie and stood up to leave, his eyes again narrowing when he glanced in her direction. After a few words with Sadie May, he left, briefly stepping aside to let a couple of cowboys pass him in the doorway.

Sadie May offered them a table by the window but they gestured towards the back of the room. Towards Charlie. Picking their way between the other patrons, they approached her table. Charlie's fingers curled around the gun in her pocket as she looked up into two trail-weary faces.

The taller of the two cleared his throat. 'Miss Charlie, it's good to see you again.'

He pulled off his hat and waited. Both in their twenties, their almost identical faces seemed familiar.

'You don't remember us, do you? Me and my brother, Bill, worked at the Crooked-W last spring after your uncle had his accident.'

In a flash, it came to her. Relief flooded through her body, making her feel almost giddy.

'I do remember. You're Carl and Bill . . . Woodard. You arrived at the same time as Al.'

'That's right. We did.'

Her breathing sounded unusually loud. 'Why don't you sit down? I could do with some company.'

They did as they were bid and, dutifully, Sadie May brought coffee.

'There's something we need to ask you,' Bill said, after exchanging a few nervous glances with his brother. 'Is everything all right?'

She waited for clarification

'What he means to say,' Carl added, swatting his brother on the arm, 'is, are you here of your own free will?'

She chuckled, taken aback. 'What do you mean?'

'Well, and we don't mean any offence, but we saw you come out of the marshal's office with that feller that was in the shootout earlier and . . . well, to be honest, he just doesn't seem like the kind of man you'd associate yourself with. After the way he dragged you out of the store, we wondered if maybe he was keeping you here against your will.'

Despite the gravity of the situation, she laughed out loud, turning a few heads. 'That was you following us?'

'We saw you and we were worried. We rode through Ranch Town a few weeks ago, saw what was left of the Crooked-W and heard what happened.' Bill shook his head, regretfully. 'Nobody seemed to know for sure what had become of you. There was a rumour you might have been kidnapped.'

'Kidnapped? No, I'm not being held

against my will and, contrary to popular belief, my friend Daniel isn't a bad man. If it wasn't for him, I'd probably be dead by now.'

The pair looked relieved and alarmed at the same time.

'Tell me, when you were in Ranch Town, did you stay at the hotel, the one run by the old lady who called herself Ma?'

Again the brothers glanced at each other.

'The hotel's gone, burned to the ground.'

Charlie gasped. 'And Ma?'

'She was badly burned when they pulled her out. She lived a couple of days but . . . '

Charlie didn't hear anything after that. Even after all the death she had seen, this one struck her like a knife through the heart. Ma had been no threat to Johnson. Burning the hotel could have been no more than an act of revenge. She was dead because of what Charlie had done to Scott.

'We pretty much rode in and rode out again,' Bill was saying. 'The whole town's like a powder keg just waiting for a spark to blow it sky high. Most decent folks had already left, the rest were packing up. To tell the truth, we didn't want to stick around once we found out the Crooked-W was gone.'

She nodded mechanically. 'I think you made the right decision.'

Daniel appeared at the window, peering in through the glass, and Charlie stood up to leave. Both men started to rise with her but she gestured them back into their seats and, after shaking each man's hand, she headed out into the street.

'They're the two that were following me,' Daniel said, meeting her at the door.

'I know. They did some work around the Crooked-W and recognized me. They got it into their heads that after what happened to the ranch, I might be in trouble. They were just looking out for me.'

He blew out his breath. 'Well at least that's two we don't have to worry about.'

She stood a minute, wondering how or whether to tell him what else she had found out. In the end, she said, 'Johnson burned Ma's hotel down.'

'And Ma?'

She shook her head, unable to say the words.

'She didn't deserve that,' he said, with real regret in his voice.

'No, she didn't. And Billy didn't. And Tom didn't. And Al didn't. And you don't. And I don't.'

She could feel the rage rising in her with every name she uttered. Daniel was talking but his words were nothing more than noise. She knew what she needed to do. Reason tried to intrude on her growing mania but she shoved it aside.

Daniel shook her gently by the shoulder.

'I'm going back to Ranch Town,' she said.

It took him a few seconds to respond. ‘I’m not saying don’t, but why?’

‘Because that’s where Val Johnson started all this and that’s where it has to end.’

31

It was a five-day ride to Ranch Town and they arrived with the grey light of dawn beginning to lighten the sky. As the steady clop of hoofs marked their passage along the main street, Daniel could make out charred timber and piles of ash where the Good Night Hotel had previously stood. Other buildings were boarded up, or simply abandoned with their doors hanging open and windows smashed.

The town lay in ruins. There was no other way to describe it.

'I wasn't expecting it to be like this,' Charlie said.

Daniel drew his horse to a stop, his gaze surveying the scene around them. 'It's a ghost town.'

'Johnson must have gone completely mad.'

They continued moving steadily

towards the Lucky Diamond where Val Johnson kept a couple of rooms on the upper floor. Nothing stirred, and leaving their horses at the empty hitch rail, they peered in through the window. A lamp burned low on the bar, casting eerie shadows around the empty room.

Keeping to one side, Daniel placed a hand on the split doors. They swung listlessly. Still nothing moved, either inside the saloon or out on the street.

Charlie pulled her gun. 'Do you think it's a trap?'

'If it was, we'd be dead by now.'

Daniel slipped the Smith & Wesson from its holster. Easing his way inside, he pulled up short to survey the scene. Tables and chairs overturned, glass showered across the floor. It looked as though Brady hadn't gone willingly.

Charlie pressed in behind him. 'What do you think happened?'

'I don't know. It's like the whole town just picked up and left. There should be someone about, don't you think?'

'It's creepy, if you ask me. Let's take a look upstairs, just to be sure.'

The steps creaked as they climbed tentatively to the first floor. Along the narrow hallway, doors were thrown open. Inside, rooms previously used for the pleasure of Lucky Diamond clients were abandoned, left in varying states of disarray. As they neared the end of the corridor, Daniel indicated that they should spread out, keeping close to the walls on either side.

The door to Val Johnson's adjoining rooms stood ajar. Before they reached it, a light inside flickered into life.

'Why don't you two lower your weapons and come on in?' a familiar voice asked.

* * *

Charlie recognized the voice instantly but it wasn't the one she was expecting. Gun firmly in hand, she pushed the door wide, squinting as she tried to see past the lamp to the man sitting behind the large desk that faced the door.

He replaced the chimney on the ornate brass lamp and pushed it aside before leaning back, resting one foot across the opposite knee as he grinned at her. 'Hello, Charlie, it's good to see you.'

'What are you doing here?' she asked.

A second man stepped from the shadows beside her. 'Did you two idiots really think you could ride into town and take on Val Johnson?'

Seeing her pa unnerved her more than she thought it would, but she was in no mood to be cowed by him. 'We killed three of your men, didn't we?'

Roy Wells scowled. 'Yes, and I should — '

He raised his hand to finish the threat but, before it fell, Daniel clamped his wrist.

'You touch her and it'll be the last thing you ever do.'

Roy's eyes narrowed as he considered the challenge. After a few seconds, he let his arm relax, dropping it loosely at his side when Daniel released it. 'No need to be like that. We're all friends here.'

Daniel grunted.

'Why don't we all sit down,' Dan Cliff suggested reasonably, 'and talk like civilized people on the same side of this trouble?'

Roy grumbled something unintelligible.

'We didn't come here to talk, Dan,' Charlie said. 'Tell us where Johnson is and we'll be on our way.'

'He's out at the Lazy-J.'

'Thanks.'

She turned abruptly but Roy's hand grabbed her arm. His fingers bit into the flesh but she didn't bend.

'I warned you,' Daniel said, prodding him in the stomach with his gun. 'Let her go.'

Roy's eyes gleamed with hostility as he took his time making up his mind.

'Best do it, Roy,' Dan advised. 'This ain't no green kid you're dealing with now.'

Roy shoved Charlie away from him, further into the room, and joined his partner behind the desk. His belligerent gaze stayed with Daniel but he held his tongue.

Dan cleared his throat. 'Daniel, I know we haven't seen eye-to-eye in the past, but I think you know I don't mean you any harm. Just give us five minutes of your time. At the very least we can tell you what you're up against. Maybe,' he said, glancing at Roy, 'we can even help you.'

Charlie laughed, but it was a hollow, mocking sound. 'Help us? If you had helped us at the start Al wouldn't be dead, Daniel wouldn't have had to kill Ralph Stanton and this town might still be home to some good people.' She choked.

'You're too late. We don't need your help now,' Daniel said, finishing for her.

Both men looked nothing short of startled.

'You killed Ralph Stanton?' Roy

asked Daniel. 'How the Hell did that happen?'

'It was him or me.'

Shaking his head in disbelief, Roy cast a sideways glance in Dan's direction but his partner was looking at his son, a smile on his lips.

'Your ma said you were quick. I guess she was right. Ralph Stanton was one man I never wanted to face down the barrel of a gun.'

'When did you talk to Ma?'

'More often than you know. Just because she didn't want me in your life didn't mean I didn't want you in mine, even if it was only through the stories she told me.' Dan sighed. 'She was a good woman, and that's why I respected her wishes and stayed away from you.'

Charlie waited for Daniel to speak but he remained tight-lipped, his face a picture of doubt and contempt.

'This is all very touching, but time's wasting,' Charlie said. 'Have you got anything useful to tell us or is this just some kind of twisted family reunion?'

'If you were a son, I'd whoop your ass for talking to us like that,' Roy said, bringing himself up short when he started forward.

'And if you had ever been a father to me, I'd give a damn.' Charlie turned and walked away. 'Go back to your hideout and do whatever it is you do best.'

Charlie heard footsteps following and steeled herself for whatever onslaught might follow. All at once she was afraid and exhilarated, breathless despite her measured steps. She wanted to run, to escape as fast as her legs would carry her, but she didn't. She just kept walking.

Outside, she and Daniel mounted their horses without a word. It seemed that they were at a place in their relationship where there was no need for words. Fate had thrown them together, but the bonds of friendship and loyalty were stronger than any blood tie.

Dan called from the balcony above them. 'You might want to get off the street. Johnson's coming, now.'

Charlie looked at Daniel. His face was white and tense. Neither of them bothered answering as they slid from their mounts. Charlie loaded the Yellow Boy and checked the rounds in her six-gun before ramming it into the holster she was wearing at her hip.

Daniel did the same with his weapons. 'Is the plan still the same?'

Looking up Charlie saw Johnson ride around the bend, ahead of a group of three rough-looking men. They rode easy in the saddle, keeping their animals to an unhurried walk. That they had seen and recognized Red and the grey was obvious when they spread out and approached the Lucky Diamond.

Charlie levered a shell into the chamber of the Yellow Boy and brought it up. 'Kill or be killed,' she said, snapping off a shot.

Another shot cracked loudly beside

her as Daniel fired almost simultaneously.

Both shots found a target and the two riders to either side of Val Johnson tumbled from their horses. It was unexpected and Johnson and the other man snatched back on the reins, grabbing for their guns. Charlie fired again, this time hitting Johnson's horse. It went down headfirst but Johnson jumped clear, returning fire as he ran across the street.

Charlie levered the Yellow Boy again and again, but somehow every shot missed him.

She felt herself grabbed by the collar as Daniel dragged her behind a water trough and slammed her down. As they reloaded, water sprayed over them, the plank walk behind splintering, but the men were firing at nothing and they knew it.

'I was hoping you'd come back to Ranch Town so I could kill you myself,' Val Johnson shouted when the gunfire stopped. 'Which one of you was it that crippled my boy?'

'It doesn't matter which of us it was,' Daniel shouted. 'You paid for two, you get two.'

Val Johnson laughed. 'How about we get this over with quickly?'

'That was the plan,' Charlie shouted, then to Daniel, 'Do you see them?'

He peered around the end of the trough, then shook his head. 'Maybe behind that trough over there. I don't know.'

She could feel her anger building, replacing the numbing fear that threatened her resolve. Taking a deep breath, she mentally pictured the street. Behind them, the saloon. Facing them, the shoemaker's and the barber's.

'I've got an idea, but it may not be a good one,' she said.

'I'm listening.'

'If they're behind that trough, then they're in front of the barber's with that big glass window. If I shoot it out, it might just surprise them enough that they do something stupid. Maybe we can draw them out.'

'It's a long shot, but it could work.' He squeezed her arm and gave her a tight smile. 'Do it.'

She fired off a shot with the Yellow Boy and the glass shattered in spectacular fashion. Johnson's man screamed, struggling to his feet as he frantically clawed at the large shard of glass protruding between his shoulder blades. As he staggered along the plank walk, Daniel's bullets cut him down.

Peering over the trough, Charlie searched for Johnson but there was no sign of him. 'Did we get him?'

'I didn't.'

'Where is he?'

Above them on the balcony, Dan called down, 'He crawled into the barber's shop. He's hiding behind the big chair.'

'Thanks,' Daniel said. 'Charlie, you lay down some cover fire while I run over there.'

'No.' She grabbed the back of his shirt, holding him back with more strength than she thought she had. 'Johnson was never your fight. I have to be the one that ends this.'

He shook his head. 'Just because you're a badman's daughter, Charlie, doesn't make you a killer.'

She wasn't angry with him. There was no condescension behind his words. The anguish in his eyes told her that it pained him to say it.

'You don't think I can do it?'

'I don't want to find out.' He leaned in and kissed her. 'Forgive me.'

'Go now,' Dan shouted, opening fire above them.

32

Daniel lurched into the street, staggering as he hunched over and zigzagged to the other side. When he slammed himself flat against the wall of the barber's shop, his gun was in his hand but he couldn't remember how it got there. He looked back but Charlie was out of sight. Belly down on the balcony above, Dan was reloading.

He eased himself to the side of the window, and listened. There was no movement, no sound that might betray the presence of the man inside but that didn't mean anything.

The minutes ticked by slowly, his mind searching fruitlessly for a way to get to Johnson without getting himself killed.

'Are you alive in there, Val?' Dan called from across the street.

'I'm alive. Just wondering what the

Hell you're doing here, Dan.'

'I'm just helping out.'

'It's not like you to take sides in a fight that doesn't concern you.'

'You didn't leave me much choice when you put that five hundred dollar bounty on my boy's head.'

Daniel heard Johnson laugh. 'I should have known. He had a look about him that I recognized but . . . I guess I must be getting old. Is he as good as you?'

'Better by all accounts. He killed Ralph Stanton.'

Daniel eased back towards the corner where an alley separated the barber's shop from its neighbour. Glancing across the street, he signalled Dan to keep Johnson talking, then ducked into it. Running to the side door, he tried the handle. Locked. He put his shoulder against it and tried to force it but it wouldn't give and he cursed under his breath.

'And the girl, she's something to Roy?' Johnson was saying.

'Daughter,' Dan answered.

With his ear pressed to the wood panels, Daniel heard Johnson swear.

'I'm telling you I didn't know that when all this started, but even if she didn't cripple my boy, she was there and didn't try to stop it. I deserve payback.'

Daniel ran back to the street. Charlie saw him immediately, as if she hadn't taken her eyes from the spot. He mouthed the word 'distraction' several times but she was struggling to understand. He pulled at his shirt, pointing towards her, and making a face that he hoped showed surprise.

Suddenly, after several attempts, she realized what he meant and nodded.

'Twenty seconds,' he mouthed, pointing to his fingers as he counted down.

He ran back to the side door.

'Scott killed my cousin, Billy,' Charlie shouted. 'He got what he deserved and as soon as you show your face you're going to get what you deserve for killing my uncle and those men at the Crooked-W.'

'A lot of men have tried to kill me, darling. I'm still standing.'

'Why not step into the street then and let a woman try?'

'That would hardly be a fair fight, would it? I think I'll just stay here until reinforcements arrive.'

Daniel placed his foot against the lock, counting. Eighteen, nineteen . . . Gunfire erupted in the street and he kicked hard. The door gave easily and he burst inside, falling over a stack of boxes and careening through the storeroom into the shop.

Johnson turned and fired but the gun was empty. He threw it at Daniel, deflecting the shot from the Smith & Wesson that was meant to kill him. Daniel's second shot hit him in the shoulder and he spun away, scrambling out through the shattered window. He crashed into Charlie who had run across the street, six-gun in hand.

She fell hard on her backside, the gun spinning away into the dirt. Johnson made a grab for it but she kicked out, her boot heel catching him a wicked blow across the wrist.

'That's enough, Johnson,' Daniel told him, jabbing the Smith & Wesson in his back.

Charlie retrieved the six-gun and clambered to her feet. Her eyes blazed in a face pale and twisted with hatred.

'Are you going to kill me now, little girl?' Johnson sneered.

Daniel tensed.

'Kill you?' she said.

Her expression oozed contempt, as she looked him over from his torn trousers to his bloody jacket, and to his injured wrist, which he cradled pitifully to his chest. Somewhere along the way, Daniel noticed, he had even lost a shoe.

If she had ever been afraid of him, she wasn't now. It showed in the gleam of her eye and the way she holstered the six-gun.

'I wanted to kill you, but then I realized that my not killing you meant more to someone else than killing you meant to me.'

She glanced at Daniel and he smiled.

'So instead, I'll watch you hang for what you've done and sleep peaceful in my bed at night knowing you've paid the price.'

The sound of voices drew their attention. Townsfolk were emerging from some of the buildings. Coming out of the saloon, Roy and Dan were herding three of Johnson's hired guns towards them, gagged and tied.

'It looks like your reinforcements have arrived,' Daniel said, shoving Johnson towards them.

He holstered his gun and moved to stand beside Charlie. Unexpectedly, she wrapped her arm around his waist and pressed in close. It felt good. Better even than he had dreamed it would be.

Johnson turned and stared at them, his piercing green eyes bright with malice. Daniel froze, his whole body seeming to tingle as he realized what was about to happen. He saw Johnson's hand snake inside his coat.

Daniel's Smith & Wesson seemed to leap into his hand, belching smoke and bullets. Johnson rocked for a second, disbelief replacing the arrogance on his face before the light left his eyes and his body crumpled to the ground.

'Boy, that was fast,' Dan said, turning him over. 'He didn't even get his gun out of the holster.'

'It looks like I was wrong about you,' Roy said. 'The way you've handled yourself today, there's a place for you with the Wells Gang, if you want it.'

Daniel shook his head. 'I hear the Crooked-W is hiring again,' he said, casting a sideways glance at Charlie. 'I think I'll stick around and see if there's a place for me there.'

'I thought you said you weren't a cowpuncher?' she reminded him.

'I'm not, but I'm sure there's something else I could do.'

She slipped her hand into his. 'In that case, let's go home, partner.'

Other titles in the Linford Western Library:

THE SIEGE OF MORTON'S CROSS

K. S. Stanley

The town leaders of Morton's Cross are awaiting with trepidation the imminent release of Dan McCleery from prison. It is common knowledge that McCleery and his gang of outlaws will want to exact revenge on the townsfolk for incarcerating him five years earlier. But in planning to survive what could become an ugly siege, the town's leaders start falling out with each other. In desperation, they hire bounty hunter Todd McFarlane. For McFarlane to outwit the slippery McCleery, however, the leaders must first step up and face their demons . . .

THE DEADLY SHADOW

Paul Bedford

In the winter of 1888, a gang led by notorious desperado Taw Johnson arrives at a small ranch near the town of Chinook. Cathy Clemens is recently married, but temporarily alone on the ranch, and Johnson makes the fateful decision to carry her off. When her husband John returns, he swears vengeance and sets off in pursuit, coldly picking the men off one by one. Against all the odds, the impressionable Cathy finds herself attracted to Johnson — and ever more alienated by her husband's unrelentingly cruel behaviour . . .

JORDAN'S CROSSING

Ethan Harker

Jack Denton is just another travel-stained wanderer when he fetches up in the town of Jordan's Crossing. There he finds a young widow, Marion Fowler, being terrorized by three men in her store, and kicks them out. But then the stakes are raised when her six-year-old son is kidnapped, and she receives a note telling her to leave the key to the store on her step. Why is there so much interest in the business — and what cost will Denton have to pay for solving the mystery and finding Marion's son?